THE LOST CITY

SEQUEL TO
TWO FACES OF THE
JAGUAR

GEORGE DISMUKES

I fondly dedicate this book to Bill Scott, one of my oldest friends, and definitely the one I have gotten into the most trouble with.
On a more serious note, Bill is the one who has always encouraged me to put my stories on paper. Had it not been for him nudging me in the right direction, this book may never have been written. May we live a hundred years, old friend!

CHAPTER ONE

The Awakening

ANDREA STOOD ALONE IN WAIST HIGH WEEDS, LOOKING UP AT the crumbling remains of the beach house at Cuyamel. The house where she had fallen in love with Brandon Shaw, and where the purpose, indeed, the mission of her life had been changed forever.

This house had been so full of life, then. The housemaids, Anna Maria and Suyapa were always up to something, chattering like two happy birds, giggling.

Not only did Anna Maria and Suyapa cook and keep the house clean, but in the days when Jungle Cargo was in full swing, Suyapa acted as the nutritionist for most of the animals brought to Jungle Cargo. She was very good at patiently feeding some baby monkey that didn't want to eat or making sure that various diets were observed with the myriad of animals.

Andrea remembered early morning breakfasts on the deck with Brandon, Lorenzo and whatever other guests might stop by. The view from the deck was like a postcard, overlooking the baby blue Caribbean. This vision of beauty was framed by coconut palms on both sides of the house.

The girls always cut lots of fresh fruit and boiled eggs which were presented on large platters. Breakfasts were filled with laughter and lots of easy chatter as everyone planned their day.

She looked to the left of the entry door, at the window of the bedroom. That bedroom is where she first surrendered herself to Brandon Shaw, and in one moment her entire life changed, for the better, she had thought. She discovered emotions she had never known before, and within them, a deeper meaning of life, a true purpose, a reason for living.

What inexplicable nightmare had happened? This is not how she and Brandon had left this house when they departed Honduras to live in Florida. Lorenzo had been here. Faithful Lorenzo, Brandon's manager of the animal compound, who Brandon had raised almost like a son. And also, the girls had been here. This was their home. They were all going to continue operating Jungle Cargo, because they had all helped give birth to the company which specialized in the export of exotic animals to the sister compound in Florida; albeit it would be a modified version of the original company. Jungle Cargo had once been a center where all exotic creatures from the forest were bought, taken in and shipped to the sister compound in Gainsville, Florida. This included almost all creatures: monkeys, birds, exotic cats and especially venomous snakes. The 'new' Jungle Cargo would be different. They planned on buying only parrots and other psittacines and making regular shipments to the United States in partnership with the owner of the Florida 'sister' compound Doug Bennett. It had all been so clear, so well planned.

So, what Andrea was seeing made no sense whatsoever, looking up at this once beautiful beach house that Brandon had built with his own hands, Lorenzo at his side working with him. It was now abandoned and falling apart? The shutters on the windows were askew, some hanging by one rusty hinge. The door was ajar. The sound of a hauntingly lonely wind whistled through the gables and carport. What possible wretched set of circumstances had made this happen?

There was no heartbeat, no life. The scene was startling, austere, stark, and most of all, alone. So desperately alone. Andrea could no longer hold her pain inside. What she saw frightened her to the core of her being. She wanted to run, but to where? She didn't know. She wanted to throw up.

Instead, she held her face in her hands and sobbed, the ache was tearing at her heart. She didn't understand. She was so alone, and she did not know the why of that either. Where was Brandon? He had promised to love her forever, to never leave her, to be by her side, no matter what life threw at them. Where was he now?

Andrea's knees felt weak. She staggered, no longer able to support her own weight. She sagged down into a kneeling position among the weeds as she bawled her eyes out. None of this made any sense. Why was it happening? What had she done wrong? What had she done to anger God?

Then, with a terrified scream, she awoke. She was covered in sweat. It had been a dream. A horrible, God forsaken nightmare. She was at home, in Florida, safe in her bedroom beside Brandon, who was sleeping peacefully. At least, until now. He stirred and said in his half sleep, "You all right?"

Andrea said nothing but nodded her head yes. Brandon smiled a sleepy smile and laid his head on the pillow to regain sleep.

Andrea sat on the side of the bed for several minutes as she continued breathing heavily, shaking, trying to bring herself back to reality and distance herself from the hellish journey her mind had taken her through. That's the trouble with dreams, she thought. They always seem so real. This one had seemed *too* damned real. And this one had frightened her right down to her core. She didn't know why, but it had.

She laid back down and snuggled as closely as she could press herself to Brandon. She wrapped one arm around him, but she was still trembling from the nightmare. She was awake, but she couldn't shake the awful, sick to her stomach feeling the dream had generated. She was frightened and she didn't know why.

But feeling the closeness of Brandon helped. Then something else inside her awoke, a primal need, and she wanted more. She gently slid her arm down and reached for Brandon's manhood. She was pleasantly surprised to discover the phase of sleep he was in had prepared him for what was quickly becoming a notion, and a desire.

For the next minute or so, Andrea manipulated Brandon until she brought him to full arousal. He was still asleep, but not for long. She gently nudged him in an effort to roll him over on his back. Then, as he started to awaken, she could wait no longer. She climbed atop her man, spread her legs wide apart and placed him against her, slowly taking him deep inside.

For the next several minutes, Andrea rode with increasing intensity until at last she reached a tumultuous, triumphant moment and all of her fears evaporated, replaced by satisfaction, reassured, safe and happy in her lover's arms.

She collapsed there, atop Brandon and did not move for several minutes, just enjoying the closeness of him, and feeling him still inside her. Now Brandon had come fully awake and as it turned out, this adventure was far from over. So, the two lovers remained connected to one another for the next hour, until both were sated and exhausted. This, Andrea thought, would be as close as she ever needed to come to Nirvana. Then she rolled off of him, to his side and quickly drifted into a peaceful sleep.

When she awoke again, Brandon was in the kitchen, preparing a repast for them to enjoy on the expansive deck behind the house. Naja was up too, sitting by the patio doors, looking out at the morning.

Somewhere in the house, a radio was turned on. Burl Ives was singing, "Have A Holly Jolly Christmas."

Andrea threw on a robe and joined Brandon in the kitchen, kissing him on the cheek and then pulled her coffee cup down from the cupboard, filling it with hot brew. She grabbed a bowl of pastries with her empty hand and followed Brandon through the patio doors out onto the deck. They placed their bowls of fruit and pastries on the round picnic table with the brightly colored umbrella. Then they sat and began surveying the morning as they ate their breakfast and sipped hot, rich coffee.

"Doesn't seem much like Christmas time here, in sub-tropical Florida," Andrea commented. "Who knows, a cold front might blow through and I'll have to put on a long-sleeved shirt."

Brandon chuckled. "Wish you were back home in Indiana?"

"No," Andrea said as she surveyed her surroundings. "But I do miss the snow at Christmas, dressing up in winter clothes, the colors of the leaves in the fall... I don't know." She sipped her coffee and then took a big bite of cheese Danish. As she chewed, she said, "Voltaire said the worst mistake we can make is to not appreciate where we are 'in the immediate'. Maybe he's right, but then again, maybe not."

"Oooh! I do believe the lady is vacillating this morning."

"My memories are very special to me. God, when you think about it, I mean, when it's all over, what else are we left with?"

"Not much, I guess." Brandon took a deep sip of coffee. "Never really gave it much thought. I'm not the philosopher you are. You are the Socrates in this family. Socrates-ette? It seems to me that you have always had this special ability to

5

think about things from a different perspective, even from a different time frame."

"What do you mean?"

"I mean, imagine in crystal clear view how a situation would be, say forty years from now. You understand?"

Just then, Naja took off down the stairs to go visit the nearby woods, the same as a housetrained dog would do. Andrea watched as the big cat trotted off into the woods. The move from Honduras had necessitated purchase of forty acres here in the Ocala National Forest, and then surrounding it with an eight-foot-high hurricane fence. It was necessary not to keep Naja in, but to keep poachers out who might spot Naja and see her as a trophy. Andrea could only imagine what kind of hell would be unleashed if Naja were to be attacked.

Naja and Brandon were not really two separate entities. They were one soul with two separate bodies.

"Do you think Naja is happy here?" Andrea asked.

Brandon thought for a moment. "Well, it's not like Honduras, where she could scamper off into the jungle and go hunting, nail an agouti, or go swimming in the river and catch a croc. But, I think overall, she's pretty content. Why do you ask?"

"I don't know. Just wondering. And what about the lord of the jungle, you? Are you happy."

"I've got you, don't I? Where are you going with this?"

"Yes, you do. And nowhere, I suppose. I was just thinking, if I occasionally miss Indiana, could you, likewise, miss Honduras?"

Brandon got a far-away look in his eyes as he sipped his coffee in silence.

Finally, he confessed over the coffee cup, "Maybe... sometimes. But we're so busy here that I don't really have time to think about it."

There was a silent pause as both of them retreated inside

their thoughts. The morning was clear. It was very early. Brandon had always been an early riser. That had been difficult for Andrea to adjust to. Much to her delight, she discovered that the minutes just past dawn are the most peaceful, so adjusting to the schedule had become easy and she welcomed it.

Naja, the sleek, three-hundred-pound jaguar, who was every bit as much a part of this household as Brandon or Andrea, returned from her sojourn to the woods. She was black as night and looked at you with golden eyes which never failed to impress, even startle those who were unaccustomed to her gaze.

Naja and Brandon were somehow connected in a way that Andrea had never seen between an animal and its master. Perhaps it had been that one factor which had made Andrea see Brandon in a different light. This because it is well known that animals have some special insight which allows them to know good people from bad people.

Her original mission to Honduras had not been to make friends with the man, much less fall in love with him and change her entire life for him. Her mission, as an undercover DEA agent had originally been to gather evidence against the jungle man so the government could arrest him, convict him and salt him away in the slammer for his participation in a drug smuggling ring.

Andrea had been determined to do just that because after all, in the beginning, this mission hadn't seemed all that different from dozens of other missions she had undertaken in other parts of the world. But then, she had been blind-sided, got caught completely off guard, faced with something totally unexpected, but admittedly, something unlike anything she had ever been confronted with before. Something that disarmed her. She found a good man wrapped inside a bad situation. A real-life quandary that seemed to echo

Shakespeare's quote: "A riddle wrapped inside a mystery, wrapped inside an enigma."

Brandon Shaw had been a legitimate exporter of exotic animals, shipping tropical livestock from Honduras to his partner in Gainsville, Florida. Brandon assimilated the animals, mostly by buying them from regional Indians who brought them to him from the jungle. His partner, Doug Bennet, operated the sister compound in Gainsville.

Doug ferried the animals from Honduras to Florida in the company plane, an old converted DC7, gutted and refitted to haul freight. In Florida, the animals were housed in a modern, well equipped compound where some were quarantined, such as psittacine birds. The ones that required no quarantine were marketed right away to zoos, pet shops, etc. It had been a small but thriving business until federal endangered species and protected animal lists began to crop up, which slowly squeezed the two partners out of business.

Brandon Shaw hit the panic button. He had nothing to fall back on. The animal business had been the only thing he had done his entire adult life. He knew no other way to make a living.

Then, when drug smugglers offered him a chance to make a lot of big money, fast, his survival instinct took control. He succumbed to temptation and accepted their insidious offer to become the transportation department of their illegal, drug smuggling enterprise.

In fairness to Brandon, it must be said that in the beginning, he didn't fully understand the horrible downstream consequences of illegal drugs, not that naivete' should be an excuse. Even so, no one but Brandon knew how badly this grated against his honor and dignity.

But there was more, so much more. And it took Andrea to discover it. When she arrived in Honduras, she found a man in torment; torn between what he knew was morally right, and the frightening prospect he found himself faced with whereby his very livelihood was drying up before his eyes. It wasn't greed that drove Brandon Shaw, but a simple desire to survive.

When, against every instinct and every tenet of her profession, Andrea fell in love with him, she was suddenly confronted with her own secret battle. First, and oddly enough, she had to deal with the guilt of allowing herself to do something so stupid as to fall in love with a man who was essentially a suspect in a drug smuggling operation. After all, by legal definition, he was one conviction away from being a criminal.

How dumb was that? she thought. It was the fuck up of all fuck ups. And so, she chastised herself, until she reached the end of her inner turmoil and admitted there was little she could do about it. It wasn't as if Andrea had volumes of experience to draw from when dealing with this kind of thing. She had only been in love once in her life and the circumstances had been a world apart from this. She had been in college. It was a typical school-girl infatuation, sweet and harmless. Well, almost harmless. She had lost her virginity to it, her purity and her innocence. But also her naivete', or so she had thought.

This feeling she had for Brandon Shaw was a whole different ball game. There was absolutely no comparison between this and a school-girl crush. This was earth shaking, life changing; and in fact, it had done just that, rattled her entire perspective about life and motives of existence. He had touched her soul without knowing it, or even trying to do so.

Once she had reached the point where she accepted there was nothing she could do to escape her love for this jungle man, her next problem became how to extricate him from the mess he had gotten himself into so that her love wouldn't have to be limited to weekly visits at the federal prison.

Brandon Shaw had really managed to get his ass in a crack

with some very bad people. As it turned out, like Julius Caesar, he was surrounded by devious enemies, some of whom pretended to be his friends, but would kill without hesitation if they didn't get their way.

In fact, one bad guy who pretended to be a friend had tried to do just that. He had tried to set a trap and kill Andrea. But she was tough, quick, well trained and smart, and it did not end well for 'Doc'. To say he wound up in hot water was an understatement. She thought back to her last vision of him, bobbing up and down in the boiling caldron of the hot spring, the flesh falling from his skull. The memory made her gorge rise.

Her next move had been to devise a comprehensive plan. To show Brandon Shaw there was a legitimate way to make a comfortable living without depending on the animal export business, or, for that matter, any other 'business' since as far as Brandon knew, Andrea had no knowledge of his illegal activities.

Then she had to persuade him to make the transition, to give up his life's work in the animal export business, *and* his new, illegal enterprise and embrace another profession; all the while keeping it a secret that (a) she was an undercover drug enforcement agent and (b) at the same time, she had to bring the shit down around the ears of the real bad guys without ever tipping Brandon about what was going on.

As if that wasn't enough, she had found herself deep in the Mosquitia jungle at an ancient Maya archaeological site known as *THE LOST CITY OF THE MONKEY GOD*, confronted with a pissed off ancient Mayan spirit who had seen fit to follow them home from the damned jungle to Cuyamel.

When it was happening, Andrea hadn't had much time to think about the incredibility of it all. Now, sitting here on this beautiful, elevated deck overlooking forty fenced-in acres in The Ocala National Forest, sipping hot coffee with her feet tucked under her, remembering those events practically knocked her out of her chair.

Therefore, it was something of an ironic lie when Brandon glanced over at her, noticed her far away gaze and asked, "What you thinking?"

She shook her head gently and said, "Nothing. Just enjoying the morning."

Just then, Andrea thought she heard Brandon's cell phone ringing. He had left it in the house, but they hadn't closed the patio doors all the way when they came out onto the deck, so the phone's ring from the living room, could be heard clearly.

"I'll get it," Andrea said, setting her coffee on the table and padding barefoot into the house.

Picking the phone up, she pressed the answer button and said, "Hello?"

A very tense sounding Lorenzo Ponce responded. "Doña Andrea? Buenos dias!"

"Lorenzo? Good morning."

"Disculpa mi. I'm sorry to disturb you so early in the morning, but I got to speak to Don Brandon. It is very important."

"Of course," Andrea said. "Just a moment."

Returning to the deck, she handed Brandon the phone. "It's Lorenzo."

"Lorenzo?" Brandon hit the button, placing Lorenzo on speaker. "Lorenzo, buenos dias!"

"Buenos dias, Don Brandon," Lorenzo replied.

"What's shaking in Honduras this morning?"

"We got a pinche' big problem down here, Jefe."

"What do you mean?"

"Bueno, I'm sure you remember that pinche' fantasma that followed you here from The Lost City."

"Yeah, I remember. It would be kind of hard to forget."

"Well, the mother is back!"

Brandon was silent as he listened. A few moments later, Lorenzo said, "You still there?"

"Yeah, I'm still here," Brandon answered. "I was just processing."

"What do you mean, processing?"

"Trying to figure out why he came back."

"I don't know. He keeps showing up all over the place, all times of the day and night. The girls are scared to death. They won't come to the house. They've gone home to Sambala. The fucking hunters won't come to the compound. They're superstitious as it is, and with this thing hanging around, they won't come within five miles of Jungle Cargo. And worse, they're telling all the other hunters. We're being put out of pinche' business, Jefe."

Brandon looked at Andrea, who sank down into the chair next to him.

"You still there, Jefe?" Lorenzo asked again.

"Yeah, yeah. I'm just trying to figure out what the damn thing wants."

"Well, I ain't no expert about spirits or anything like that, but I think it's looking for you."

"Me? What the hell for?"

"Don't ask me. I don't know nothing about pinche' ghosts. You gotta take that up with the pinche' fantasma."

Suddenly, Andrea spoke up. "I hate to say it, but it makes sense. I think the reason that thing followed Antonio is because 'it' saw Antonio with you. Maybe it figured that if it stayed with him, that would lead to you. Then it showed up at the compound and caused...well, we all know what it caused. Like it or not, you've got some unfinished business with that thing, Lover."

"What?" Brandon said incredulously.

"Yep. I repeat, like it or not."

"Well, I goddamn sure don't like it!" Brandon turned back to the phone. "Where are you now, Lorenzo?"

"I'm at my primo's house in Sambala. Hell, I ain't going to Cuyamel either. I don't know what that thing might do if it gets pissed off."

"No. Of course not. Alright, stay where you are and play it safe. I need to think about this and talk it over with Andrea. We'll get back to you before the day is out."

"Bueno, pues. I think there are several cold beers here with my name on them. Me and my primo are gonna do some catching up."

"Okay, good. Don't forget the limes and salt! Talk to you this afternoon. Good hearing your voice, although I wish it had been for another reason."

With that, Brandon hit the 'End' button and disconnected the call.

He immediately turned to Andrea. "What do you mean, I've got some 'unfinished business', with a frigging Maya spirit? How can you have any kind of 'business' with a spirit at all? That's crazy."

"Maybe. But then again, maybe not as crazy as you think. Look, when we first encountered that thing at The Lost City of The Monkey God, *it* was the one who looked like it had seen a ghost when it looked at you. It supplicated itself to you, fell down on its hands and knees. Then it tried to hand you that scepter."

"Yeah. So what?"

"Just stay with me for a minute. The next thing we know, it's trying to hitch a ride in a helicopter. Now tragically, that turned out bad."

"Two innocent people died. Bad is hardly the word," Brandon interjected.

"True enough. But I have always wondered why it wound up

on that helicopter to begin with. Are spirits by nature malevolent? Everything I have ever heard suggests that when spirits get stirred up it's because something has disturbed their peace, so to speak. That has certainly got to apply in The Lost City of The Monkey God, where several dozen archaeologists are tearing around the site, digging things up, knocking holes into the sides of pyramids. If I were a ghost, I guarantee you, I'd be pissed off."

"Andrea! You sound like you've been reading too many comic books."

"Look, Brandon, you damn near killed me when you were possessed by that 'thing.' If that snake pit had still been in use, we wouldn't be having this conversation. Now, excuse me, but I've done a certain amount of thinking about it since that night. Not that I've wanted to, God knows. But you've got to admit, it was a pretty traumatic moment for us all."

"Yeah, I guess so."

"And the worst part about it was, it *was* real; not comic book stuff, but real."

Brandon thought about Andrea's words for a long while. Finally, "Okay, where are you going with this? And what are we going to do to save Lorenzo's ass, along with Jungle Cargo?"

Andrea stood up and looked into Brandon's eyes. "You've got to go back…*we* have got to go back. We're going back to Jungle Cargo, and probably back to The Lost City of The Monkey God. I'm as sure of it as I am sure that your eyes are blue."

Naja looked up at the two humans as if she understood every word.

Brandon stared at Naja, then at Andrea. "Merry Christmas!" he said resignedly.

Andrea picked up the phone and called Doug Bennett. When Doug answered, Andrea said, "Doug, we need to hitch a ride on the company plane!"

CHAPTER TWO

Return to Jungle Cargo

WHEN ANDREA, BRANDON, NAJA AND DOUG BENNETT DROVE though the archway which declared they were at Jungle Cargo, everything was very still and eerie. A thick fog hugged the ground, lending a very other-worldly atmosphere. Brandon came very close to the house with the Jeep before he could see it and stop.

Naja was the first one to hop out of the Jeep, sniffing around, doing recon for her master, making sure the area was secure. Jungle Cargo was abandoned, much as Andrea had seen it in her dream. The house was not in disrepair the way she had dreamed, and there were no high weeds, but the feeling of stark abandonment prevailed, and it was un-nerving. Andrea stepped out of the Jeep, but even before she had walked a step, something overcame her.

A feeling of despair suddenly cocooned Andrea and she staggered.

"What's wrong?" Brandon asked.

"A...a feeling of deep melancholy. Very pervasive, overwhelming. I sense sadness, hopelessness, loss. No answers, only questions."

"What question?"

"Where am I?"

Brandon watched Andrea, and listened, but said nothing.

As Brandon dismounted the Jeep, his and Andrea's words, which they had discussed prior to leaving Florida, kept replaying in his mind.

"We can't just 'go down there'. We need a plan."

"Yes, I agree, Brandon, but what kind of plan can you put in place to confront an ancient spirit? Should we work on the theory that it wants something specific? And if so, what does it want?"

Brandon shook his head. "I don't know. I just don't know. I'm new at this sort of thing. I didn't even believe that ghosts existed before encountering this frigging thing in the Lost City. I'm still not sure I believe it. It's just too much...crossing over into the other world, bullshit. A fucking green ghost that looks like an ancient Mayan chieftain? And so far, it's killed at least two people that we know of, maybe more. Remember Pablo Palma? What if it decides it wants to kill us?"

"I know. That thought has crossed my mind. But Lorenzo needs help. What do we do, leave him hanging out on a limb?"

"No, of course not," Brandon protested. "We can't do that. Lorenzo is like the son I never had. I can't and won't abandon him when he needs me the most, and I know you won't either."

"Neither will Naja," Andrea said as she bent over to scratch Naha, reassuringly. "So...we're going?"

"Yes, we're going, just as you predicted. I guess we'll figure out what to do when we get there. Christ-o-mighty. Just what I need, a fucking ghost in my life! I must be crazy as a bed bug."

The words swirled around in Brandon's head, but offered no comfort, much less answers, and now, here he was, standing in front of the house at Cuyamel, the house he built with his own hands, and with the help of Lorenzo. He stood, feeling a little lost, looking up at the back door, wondering what he was going to find inside. But for the moment, his woman was staggering. He went to her to hold her, give her physical and emotional support.

But 'up there' awaited. As if reading his mind, Naja made her way up the stairs, sniffing carefully as she went. Andrea stood beside Brandon. She was armed with her Glock, but she felt a little stupid. What good would a pistol be against a damned spirit?

"Well," Brandon said, "into the breach." He approached the bottom landing and carefully climbed the stairs leading up to the back door of the house. It was no surprise to discover the door was unlocked. But the house was just as it appeared, empty of any human occupation.

Brandon swung the door open wide. Naja was the first to enter, seeming to revel in revisiting her old home. She was blissfully unaware of any poltergeists but seemed a little confused at the house being empty. She was used to there always being activity here, the sounds of feet on the wooden floors, laughter, someone fussing at her for getting into one of the cabinets or the larder. Music. But now, there was nothing. Just a six inch long Honduran scorpion crawling along the wall which Brandon spotted and crushed with a magazine.

Andrea appeared in the doorway. She had crept silently up the stairs and now peeked in as Brandon and Naja surveyed the empty house.

"Well, no one's here," Brandon said softly, almost to himself. "Apparently not even that pesky ghost."

"I don't like this," Andrea said. "The house seems so desolate, almost like my dream."

"What dream?" Brandon asked, looking up at her.

"Just a dream I had. No matter. Dreams are all crazy."

Doug Bennett appeared in the doorway, stopping to peek around before entering. "I've got to say," he stammered, "these stories you two have, uh, regaled me with, uh, about a Mayan ghost, um, um. It all sounds like you've been getting into the same bottle of bad booze."

"I wish that's all it was, partner," Brandon said as he made his way slowly through the house.

The four went through the house, investigating each room. Somehow, the house seemed to have a hollow sound which echoed with each footstep.

"God!" Andrea returned to the living-room and sat on the sofa, her Glock still in her right hand. "This house has always been so full of life. So warm, so welcoming. Most of the time things were very happy. Sometimes not. But there was always sounds of something going on. I don't like this. It isn't natural. You can smell the fear."

"Smell the fear?" Doug said. "Is that what I'm uh, smelling, fear?"

"Smell the fear," Brandon added. "Well, when you stop to think about it, I guess we're the ghost busters because we've got to figure out what to do to restore things to normal around here."

Andrea looked at Brandon disdainfully. "'Ghost busters'? Oh, please! I could have done without putting that label on it." She holstered her pistol.

"Label or not, we've got to devise a plan, which I believe I wanted to do before we left Florida, if you'll remember. Now, we've had an opportunity to see the result of the problem close up. So, what the hell are we going to do about it? I mean, we've got to basically get rid of that fucking ghost. How does one, in reality, go about evicting a ghost?"

"I don't know, Brandon. I've had enough to do just keeping up with day to day stuff."

"You know," Brandon admitted, "I never told you this, but I did have one other 'ghostly experience' in my life. It was many years ago. I was at Tikal in northern Guatemala, the Peten Jungle. Tikal is a major archaeological site with two huge pyramids facing each other. The Pyramid of The Giant Jaguar and the other one, facing that one from about a hundred yards away that they just call, 'Temple 2'.

"Anyway, I was in Temple 2, exploring the interior chambers of the temple on top of the pyramid. It started raining. I mean, really raining, as in a jungle downpour. There was no way I was going to try to go down those steep slippery steps in the rain. So, I made myself comfortable, sitting cross legged in the doorway, looking out at the rain pattering on the jungle canopy and smelling the fresh air. It was kind of relaxing.

"Then, all of a sudden, I heard these voices coming from behind me. It was weird because I had already been back there in the inner chamber, just a couple of minutes ago and nobody except me and some bats had been there. Still, I got up and returned to the inner chamber to check. I was completely alone, but I still heard the voices. I thought, oh shit, somebody got trapped outside around on the backside of this thing and can't make it to the front in the rain. Then I started listening closer. I thought I recognized the language, but just a word here and there. Whoever was yakking their mouth was doing it in Mayan.

"Anyway, after the rain let up, I made my way around the outside of the temple to the back side. Nobody was there. It was just me. I made my way down the side of the pyramid, but the longer I thought about that incident, the more it gave me the willies. Now we're faced with this. It makes me realize I probably wasn't hallucinating in Temple 2. I am now sure I was hearing the voices of ghosts. Maybe even Stormy Sky, an old ruler of Tikal. I mean, he would be the most logical one to be up there in the temple."

Andrea and Doug looked at one another, then back at Brandon.

Brandon stood there for a long moment, thinking back,

remembering. Then, "Okay, that's it. You don't know what the hell to do. I sure don't know. We need a crash course in ghosts. The more we learn about them, the better we'll be able to deal with this nuisance."

Andrea thought about Brandon's words. "That's very logical, lover. But where do we learn about ghosts?"

Brandon smiled an ironic smile, out the corner of his mouth. "From people who believe in them. People who have believed in them for a long time. The Quiche' Maya are the ones who wrote the Popol Vuh, which is a Mayan version of a Bible. Now, to me, the Popol Vuh is one hundred percent, unadulterated horseshit. But it might be time to take a second look."

"You think our answers are in the Popol Vuh?" Andrea asked.

"No," Brandon said, "But descendants of the people who wrote the Popol Vuh are still alive and well today, living in the Alta Verapaz, the high mountains of Guatemala. And if tradition holds true, they're just as full of ghost lore horseshit as their ancestors.

"Guatemala? Are we going to Guatemala?"

"Just as fast as we can get there," Brandon said with a look of destiny on his face. "We're going to a place called Chichicastenango."

"Never heard of it."

"Oh, you're gonna love it there. They've got the damdest market you ever laid eyes on. Let's go."

"Not so fast!" Andrea said, as she stroked Naja. "What are we going to do with Naja? She might be a little hard to get through Guatemalan customs."

"We're going to leave her with Lorenzo and Doug. Doug, you don't mind holding down the fort here for a few days, do you?" Brandon asked.

"Do I have a choice?"

"No. Not really. Come on, everybody. We've got to make a quick trip to Sambala before we can go anywhere else. We've got to dig Lorenzo out of that Palapa bar and sober him up."

———

The reunion with Lorenzo was a mix of emotions. Brandon's faithful compound manager rose from the table where he was sitting and getting drunk to greet his boss with an abrazo. Both men were glad to see each other, but the circumstances managed to distract from what otherwise would have been a back slapping, hoorah. Although Brandon's compound manager was overjoyed to see his old boss, plus Doug and Andrea, he was consumed with worry and fear over the problem at hand, which of course was the apparition. He was also half in the bag from sitting in a palapa bar on the beach with his cousin and soaking up Honduran beer.

Beers were ordered for everybody, plus a saucer of key limes cut into wedges. Then, as they drank cold beer, Brandon explained his plan to Lorenzo and asked that he join with Doug and baby sit Naja. Lorenzo loved the big cat, so he readily agreed. In fact, most people in Sambala knew Naja, so she would be a welcome visitor.

After instructing Lorenzo to sober up and have faith that the problem would be solved, he gave Lorenzo another big reassuring abrazo and then explained things to Naja in a language that only she understood. She would be staying there, with Lorenzo. Brandon needed the jaguar to be on her best behavior until he returned.

After that, Brandon and Andrea took their leave and departed the small village. Doug drove them to the La Ceiba airport where they booked a flight on TACA Airlines to Guatemala City.

CHAPTER THREE

Trip into the Clouds

THAT WOULD BE THE CLOSEST AIRPORT TO CHICHICASTENANGO. The last leg of the trip would be by rented vehicle up winding mountain roads which found their way higher than the clouds. But that part of the trip would be slated for the following day. There was no way in hell Brandon would drive on Central American roads after dark, much less the winding mountain roads leading to the cloud city.

Once Brandon and Andrea landed in Guatemala, they cleared immigration and customs, then rented a vehicle and drove into downtown Guatemala City. Once there, they secured a nice room at the elegant Hotel Tropical Maya, where they settled in and, for the moment at least, put their mission and their worries aside.

The trip had been exhausting, both emotionally and physically. A hot bath was in order, followed by a relaxing, sumptuous dinner in the elegantly appointed dining room of the hotel. The muted dining room was complete with a grand piano and a skilled piano player was softly playing an intermezzo.

They dined on traditional Guatemalan chicken pepi'an,

and a bottle of Merlot. Dinner was relaxing, but in the back of their minds, both Brandon and Andrea knew they had better savor this moment as best they could, because what was ahead of them was going to be anything but relaxing. Indeed, the chances were, it would try their souls.

Maybe that was part of the reason, when they returned to the room following the beautiful dinner, that they held each other tightly and passionately. It was now time to satisfy another hunger. A sweet hunger that neither of them could ever get enough of.

———

The next morning, the intrepid duo headed out of Guatemala City in the blue Jeep-like vehicle they had rented, toward the winding, uphill road that led to Chichicastenango. As the crow flies, the town is barely seventy-five clicks away from Guatemala City. Via road it is a little over one hundred and forty-five kms. And all of that, is uphill, most of it *steeply* uphill, with mountain road curves so sharp you can kiss your own elbow going around them.

To say this road is dangerous would satisfy the understatement for the year. Trucks and busses often miss the steep, graded curves and wind up careening into verancas hundreds of feet below. The road is dotted at every bend with flower embossed crosses, commemorating the loss of loved ones who took an ill-fated ride. Brandon had been on this, and other roads like it in Central America more times than he could count, but never on public transportation. Nor would he ever. Despite his former profession and enterprise with poisonous snakes, he had never held a death wish. In his opinion, only people who viewed death as inevitable would chance a ride on a Central American bus.

Andrea clutched the handhold on her side of the vehicle

tightly. Her stomach was nauseated from the constant turning back and forth, to say nothing of the thinning air. At one point, they spotted a place to pull off the road for a minute and she pleaded with Brandon to do just that.

"Please, honey. If you don't, I'm going to lose my breakfast."

Brandon gladly obliged.

The view from the roadside cantil overlooked a lush, verdant rain forest shrouded valley, surrounded by steep mountain sides. It was postcard beautiful, and standing beside the vehicle, Andrea enjoyed breathing in the cool, sweet, oxygen-rich fresh air.

They were surrounded by a symphony of sounds emitted from the mountain rainforest, monkeys and tropical birds, including the rare quetzal, the exotic bird from which the ancient Maya extracted colorful tail plumes for their chieftains' elaborate head-dresses. In ancient times as well as modern day, the quetzal was considered royal and it was forbidden to kill one. They could be trapped, and their tail feathers plucked, but then they had to be released.

In modern day Guatemala, the quetzal has lent its name and image to the national currency, and it is still considered royal, protected and untouchable. The penalty for harming one is as steep as the mountainsides where they abide.

Andrea was so hypnotized by this vista that she was reluctant to get back into the vehicle. But remount she must, for somewhere ahead, above the clouds, Chichicastenango awaited them, as well as the object of their mission. Before getting in the vehicle however, she looked around and tried to absorb one last memory. This place had magic. As she visually panned the scene, she felt like she was watching a 3D movie. It was very hard to stop looking as she climbed backed into her seat.

Onward and upward they went, grinding gears and

winding around razor sharp curves, passing trucks with noisy mufflers that billowed black smoke along the narrow road. These were trucks which had delivered their cargo to Chichicastenango, and were outbound, headed down, out of the cloud mountains toward Guatemala City.

Eventually, they approached Chichicastenango. Andrea began seeing Maya Indians walking beside the road. The women were attired in extremely colorful homespun blouses made of bright red and blue and yellow cloth, called Huipils. The men wore equally colorful trousers called pantalones. Brandon explained that not unlike the tartans of Scotland, each family clan had its own special pattern and a person's family affiliation could be identified by their huipil.

Andrea's apprehension, caused by the nightmare road, evaporated and was suddenly replaced with awe and excitement at seeing such amazingly beautiful costumes and odd things the Indians carried, often-times on their heads. Things such as heavy clay urns filled with water, cooking oil, or kerosene to heat their homes.

This was an amazing world. She had not expected such beauty. It was a crystal ball- glimpse into the past. These were the Quiche' Maya. And they had been here for thousands of years. In many ways, not much had changed during that time.

By the time they reached Chichicastenango proper, Andrea was enthralled, and anxious to check into the hotel, then explore this fascinating town high in the Alta Verapaz mountains of Guatemala. She was very glad she had brought her camera. Smiling to herself, she knew it would get a lot of use this day!

In fact, Andrea almost hit sensory overload. After checking into the Hotel Cielo Azul and getting settled in, it was a short walk to one of the many markets in Chichi (the nickname for Chichicastenango) where Andrea began her photo safari.

Andrea found herself surrounded by open air shops filled

to the rafters with brightly colored cloth items. Material the Maya referred to as "Tela" was made into clothing, tablecloths, table runners, curtains. This cloth wasn't something the Maya bought. They grew the cotton, then twilled it into thread, dyed the thread and loomed the cloth. Andrea thought this was the way it must have been in antiquity. She took many pictures of women looming cloth, but discovered it was the men who sewed the various products.

Andrea was beside herself, photographing a thousand other things, straw items, leather items, things carved from stone. There was clay pottery, ceremonial masks carved of wood and brightly painted. There were street vendors selling tacos, and sandwiches called 'pupusas'. But above all, there was color. And not just with cloth.

She also discovered that the Maya love flowers. There were flower vendors everywhere. Andrea was beside herself to discover she could buy an entire spray of flowers for only a couple of Quetzal.

"This is amazing," she commented to Brandon while admiring a particularly beautiful bunch of gladiolas. "In the United States, flowers are used for occasional decoration. Here, they are a basic part of life. The Maya must have beautiful souls. I am so glad you brought me here, Brandon. I never dreamed such a world existed. It's as if we have traveled through a portal in time to a different world."

She took hundreds of pictures of everything she saw in Chichi—people, buildings, the marketplaces, the flowers, the flower vendors. She was in love with a place such as she had never dreamed of. She also loved the gentle people but couldn't get over the fact that the average height of a Maya woman was barely five feet, with the men being only a couple of inches taller. She saw living history, and it touched her heart.

By the same token, the Maya also noticed Andrea. They were unaccustomed to seeing blond hair and many Indian women asked if they could touch Andrea's long, blond hair, because they thought the sun had touched her and made her hair that color. Delighted to comply, it was now Brandon's turn to take the camera and photograph Andrea communicating with the Maya.

She was also enthralled by the Church of Santo Tomas, painted chalk white, with broad steps leading up to the landing. And there, on the landing sat a Mayan "curandero," or witch doctor, burning incense, a practice allowed by the Catholic Church, who had enough sense to allow the Maya to practice their own rituals, even in the shadow of the church.

Typically, on a Sunday, Maya Indians would attend their Indian rituals, and then attend Catholic mass. The Catholic church would not change them. Their ancestors had been here long before the Spaniards introduced any Christian religion. The only thing to do if they wanted to keep the peace was to let them worship both religions and that was easy, for the Maya are a very devout people.

Lunchtime found Brandon and Andrea in the Café Cacique where Andrea chatted like an excited child as they awaited their meals to be served. They had ordered a type of roast pork with chili sauce and rice on the side. It was moist, rich and delicious. They washed it down with fruit juice.

"Coming here is like an awakening," Andrea said, excitedly, not being able to stop talking about her new discovery. "It's…a spiritual experience, a journey through time. My God, looking at these people, I can see very clearly into the past, perhaps a thousand years."

Brandon looked at his enthusiastic woman but said nothing. He thought he understood what she was feeling. It would be impossible to see these beautiful people and not feel something deep inside.

They had finished their meal and were just sitting at the table, relaxing, chatting, allowing their meal to settle a little before continuing their exploration of Chichi; when an old Mayan man who looked to be in his late sixties, using a walking stick and dressed in typical Mayan pantalone', and old leather sandals entered the café. He spotted Brandon and Andrea, then walked directly over to their table and sat down in the available chair. He was unmistakably Quiche'. His face was deeply wrinkled, his skin looked like old leather, His eye sockets were sunken, and his eyes were so dark brown, they were almost black.

"My name is Kan-Bah," he said unceremoniously, and with a distinct Indian accent, looking Brandon straight in the eyes. "You have here to Chichicastenango looking for me."

"What?" Brandon said, completely taken aback.

The old Maya continued to sit in the chair, unblinking, saying nothing; just staring at Brandon.

Brandon finally managed to stammer, "Who are you?"

"I am Kan-Bah," the old Maya repeated.

"Well, excuse me, but that doesn't help a lot. What is it you want?"

"It is not what I want, Don Brandon Shaw. It is what you want, and what you need, and what you must have."

"How do you know anything about what I want? Or for that matter, what I need?" Brandon demanded. Kan-Bah said nothing. He just continued to stare.

Brandon stared back, perplexed, his patience starting to wear thin. "Excuse me, Señor, whatever your name is, but you're starting to piss me off."

"That would be a waste of time, and more than a little pendejo," Kan-Bah said in a flat, unemotional tone. "Did you and the beautiful Doña Andrea not come here in search of someone to help you with the duende that besieges you? Where did you think you would find this person you seek, and how? I have been watching you explore our beautiful village. But now the time has come to speak of your problem."

Brandon and Andrea looked at each other. "I don't, I don't understand," he said to Kan-Bah. "We just got here. I haven't told a soul why we are here. How would you know?"

"I am Kan-Bah. And I know that the duende wants to be rid of you as badly as you want to be rid of it."

Brandon sat back and thought about Kan-Bah's words, while visually checking with Andrea several times to gauge her reactions to this old man, and what he was saying. But repeated eye contact with her was absolutely no help. She looked as much at a loss as he felt.

"Okay," Brandon finally managed to stammer. "We'll play your game…for now. What's next?"

"It is no game. If you want to solve your problem, we leave in the morning. I will be at your hotel waiting for you in the lobby, muy temprano. At daybreak. I will go with you to Cuyamel, and then we must all go to The Lost City of The Monkey God, together."

"Well, now, not so fast," Brandon said. "I need to know how much you're gonna want for this service?"

Kan-Bah looked at Brandon as he rose from his chair, using his walking stick for support. "Would you put a price on your eternal soul?"

"What?"

"That is what is at stake, Don Brandon Shaw. The answer is, your money is of no use to me. I'll see you in the morning."

With that, Kan-Bah shuffled out of the restaurant, around the corner, out of sight. He was gone as quickly as he had come, leaving Brandon and Andrea speechless. Brandon had goosebumps on his arms.

Andrea looked over at him. "Brandon?"

"Don't ask." He looked back at her. "I have no answers. But I'll tell you one thing, that is just about the scariest, most weird thing that has ever happened to me; and in *my* life, I've had some pretty weird things happen!"

The rest of the day was spent trying to regain normalcy. Andrea had spotted several things in the market during her first walk through that she wanted to buy, but didn't, because she was so involved in photo documenting every blessed thing she saw. She had promised herself to double back and now she was doing that, but she was still thinking about the mysterious Kan-Bah. It was impossible not to.

Questions swirled through her head, non-stop. How did Kan-Bah know she and Brandon were in Chichicastenango? How did Kan-Bah know what they wanted? When she occasionally glanced over at Brandon, it was obvious that he was pondering the same things. When they stopped for refreshments in a small sidewalk café, Brandon finally gave voice to his wrinkle-browed thoughts.

"I think both of us are worried about the same thing," he began. "But perhaps 'worry' is not the right word or attitude. Whoever Kan-Bah is, whatever he is, I think he has come to help us."

"You think so? Wait a second. You are by nature the most suspicious person I have ever known. Now you're going to tell me that you're ready to go off into the deep jungle with some goober that we just met without knowing a thing about him?

Brandon rose and started pacing the sidewalk. "I don't know what the hell to do. I'm in uncharted territory here. I've never dealt with spirits or people who know about spirits. I'm blindfolded, throwing darts at a wall. All I'm going by at this point is, I don't sense any malevolence about him. In fact, just the opposite. There seems to be something about him that is, clean, like fresh air. Does that make any sense? He's old. There should be something musty about him, but there isn't."

Andrea reluctantly nodded agreement. "That's kind of weird," she said, looking away, at nothing.

Brandon continued. "My guess is, he's a Quiche' curandero. The Quiche have a reputation for tinkering around with, I guess what you would call...'the spirit world'. I've always considered it ten yards of Maya Indian horseshit. But maybe it's time to take a second look."

"Perhaps!" Andrea said, thoughtfully. "Now that our lives apparently depend on it."

"Yes," Brandon said with a half-smile, trying to lighten the situation and mood. "Now that our asses are more up against the wall than at any other time in our lives! The only thing that sticks in my craw is, why? Why would this character care about helping complete strangers? He doesn't know us." Brandon resumed his seat.

"I think I know the answer," Andrea said. "The answer lies in who he is. He comes from a different worldview. You and I make decisions and judgements based on the assumption that everyone is more or less like us. Therefore, they must place the same value on the same things that we do. I get the impression that Kan-Bah comes from a different world. Granted, I'm not sure what world that is, but it obviously is not a dimension that we would understand. Does that help answer your question?"

"Not a bit!" Brandon said. "But you may have stumbled onto something with the word 'dimension'." Then Brandon rose from his seat and helped Andrea to get up from where she sat, so they could continue their shopping.

As they strolled, Brandon said, "You know, what you said sounds real good. I think I should have read it somewhere!"

Andrea laughed and put her arm around his shoulder.

———

It was hardly a surprise that when Brandon and Andrea arrived at the lobby of their hotel the next morning at dawn, packed and ready to go, Kan-Bah stood there, waiting for them, stoic, silent, walking stick in hand, although he was not altogether unfriendly. He did manage a brief smile at one point, when he saw how many packages Andrea had accumulated in the marketplaces of Chichicastenango.

Brandon and Andrea greeted Kan Bah and tried to show him as much warmth as possible. But Kan-Bah was still an unknown equation. A stranger who had mysteriously appeared in their lives and yet, seemed to know every detail of their quandary. How he knew was 'the mystery'. Why he wanted to stick his neck out for strangers was an equally befuddling mystery.

Andrea got the impression as she watched Kan-Bah climb into the back seat of the vehicle that he may not have ever ridden in a car before. He was certainly confused by the seat belt, which Andrea had to stretch across him and buckle.

"It's for your safety," she explained with a smile.

And the airport was an entire other story unto itself. The old Indian could scarlessly disguise his confusion from seeing this world completely unknown to him. He tried his best to maintain his stoic persona. But that was hard to do while at the same time taking in and absorbing so many things he had never seen before, and the chances were, he had never imagined.

Yet, when the plane lifted off from the runway, he stared out the window, completely at ease.

Less than twelve hours later, the trio pulled up in front of Jungle Cargo, at Cuyamel. Doug, Lorenzo and Naja were there, as well as the girls, Anna Maria and Suyapa, waiting for them. When they disembarked, Naja, not unlike a huge housecat rubbed against Brandon legs, and then went to Andrea. Kan-Bah smiled but was otherwise somehow removed and mysterious. He did not seem surprised to see Naja.

The breeze blew fresh, coming in from the Caribbean, which was only scant yards away, in front of the house. The sound of waves could be heard washing up on the beach. Introductions were offered between Doug, Lorenzo Anna Maria, Suyapa and Kan-Bah. There were welcoming hugs between Lorenzo and Andrea, then Brandon, and of course the girls.

Kan-Bah walked closer to the house and stood apart from the rest of the group. After a minute he said, "The duende 'no esta aqui'. He is not here at this moment."

"Don't worry," Lorenzo said. "He will be. He shows up at all hours. There's no rhyme or reason to it."

Kan-Bah looked puzzled for the first time. "Rhyme or reason? I do not understand."

"Oh! It means like, unpredictable. There's no telling when it might appear, or where for that matter. But the most frequent place seems to be on the front deck, just outside the patio doors."

"Then we should go there," Kan-Bah said. "Show me this place."

"Absolutely. My pleasure," Lorenzo said, and gestured toward the stairs. As Kan-Bah ascended the staircase and entered the house, Lorenzo turned to Brandon and Andrea and whispered, "Who the fuck is this guy?"

"We don't know," Brandon answered truthfully, looking in the direction Kan-Bah had taken.

"Oh good! You don't know?" Lorenzo said quizzically. "You don't know? You brought this weirdo here and you don't... never mind. Great! Just pinche' great! Okay...well, let me follow this puto and show him where the duende is making its most frequent appearance. Don't know? Hijo de la chingada!" With that, Lorenzo bounded up the stairs.

Brandon bent down to hug Naja and give her some much needed attention. She mewed softly, rubbing her head against Brandon's arm and chest. She had obviously missed her master. After a minute of this, Doug, Brandon and Andrea ascended the back steps leading into the house, followed closely by the jungle cat.

They found Lorenzo standing next to Kan-Bah, just outside the patio doors, on the deck. Kan-Bah was looking with some satisfaction at the ocean. When he sensed the group of people near him, he smiled and said, "This is something one doesn't get to see in the Alta Verapaz."

"Beautiful, isn't it?" Brandon commented.

"Yes, it is," Kan-Bah nodded his head. "Most places on earth have their own special kind of beauty, if only man takes time to appreciate them. In the Alta Verapaz, there is Lake Atitlan which rests in the crater of an ancient volcano. It is beautiful, but not like this. It is very different. There is something wild and untamed, something very dangerous about this beautiful water."

Reflecting on those words, the small gathering stared out at the sea, not speaking for the next few minutes. Then Kan-Bah turned and walked back into the house.

"Do you suppose somebody could make some coffee?" He asked.

"Right away," Lorenzo responded, and set about preparing a pot of coffee. Truth be told, it felt good to Lorenzo to do something…anything, to bring this house back to life, out of hibernation.

By evening, the house was approaching normalcy. Lorenzo had made a quick trip to Sambala and fetched some supplies, then stopped at the village trucha for beer. By dinnertime, there was fruit on the kitchen bar and the girls were making tortillas for tacos.

As Kan-Bah ate, he calmly talked to everyone, saying, "When the duende manifests itself, do not be alarmed. Spirits are like wild animals, they feed off of your emotions. If he senses fear, he will react to that. If he senses calm, he will react to that equally."

"Why is the duende coming here?" Andrea asked.

"Don't you know?" Kan-Bah answered. "He seeks this man of yours, Don Brandon Shaw."

"But why?"

"I have my suspicions," Kan-Bah said. "But I won't be sure until the duende makes itself known."

"That's just terrific," Brandon said, now slightly upset, getting up to pace back and forth. "I've got a fucking ancient Mayan ghost crawling up my ass, and we don't know the reason why." He then exited through the patio doors onto the deck and walked to the railing, where he stood alone, looking out at the sea.

Andrea watched him. One part of her wanted to go to him, to join him there and put her arm around him to offer some degree of comfort. But she knew Brandon Shaw. And she knew he was pondering things alone for the moment. Going to him would do no good. It would only be a distraction. Kan-Bah sat calmly at the table and ate his dinner with dignity, and in silence.

Only Naja approached the jungle man. Under no circumstance was she ever prohibited from being with Brandon. As so often demonstrated, it was as if their souls were connected. And it was not a thing overlooked by Kan-Bah. He watched with intense interest, the interaction between the jungle cat and her master. Indeed, judging from his expression, it was if he gleaned information from the display of affections.

But Brandon Shaw wasn't just daydreaming He was watching an older man, perhaps in his sixties, walking along the beach. He had never seen the man before, but he looked like an American. He carried a walking stick and seemed in no hurry, just enjoying the evening. He spotted Brandon at the railing, paused and waved at him with a friendly smile. Brandon waved back. The man continued down the beach, stopping frequently to pick up a seashell and inspect it.

Meanwhile, Lorenzo, unable to contain his curiosity about Kan-Bah, pulled his chair a little closer to the old Mayan, leaned over to him and asked, "Please excuse my curiosity, but who are you? Or maybe the question is, what are you?"

Kan-Bah looked straight ahead, unflustered by Lorenzo's probing question. "I am Kan-Bah."

"Yeah," Lorenzo pressed. "I heard that part. But are you a curandero, or what?"

Kan-Bah turned his head to stare at Lorenzo with disdain. "A curandero?" Kah-Bah said the word like he was spitting sand out of his mouth. "Curanderos are, I believe your term is, snake oil salesmen. They are pendejos relying on the stupidity of other pendejos to make a living."

Lorenzo nodded agreement. "Well, I will have to agree, that is always what I have thought. It's kind of refreshing to hear someone else say it. So, if that is what you are *not*. What is it that you are?"

"I am Kan-Bah. There is no name for what I do, no word. Why does there always have to be a label? A title? When you meet somebody, the person will say, 'This is Don Alejandro. He is…a rancher. He is a suit maker. He is a doctor.' I am Kan-Bah. I suppose, if it will help you, I have been called, 'A Viejo Viajero'."

"A Viejo Viajero? Old Traveler?"

"What difference does it make what I am called? The reason for my coming here is at hand. That is the only thing of importance."

"Which is…?"

"I am here to help you. And I am here to help the duende."

"Help the duende? What do you mean, help the pinche' duende?"

"Do you imagine that you are the only ones in pain? I sense great suffering by the duende. This is a place of unrest, unhappiness, brought on by deep anxiety, deep pain. We have to find out why and see if we can help him. Then, maybe he will leave you alone. Did you think you would conquer him? Is that how you would fix the problem? You can't 'conquer' a duende. If you tried, he would vanquish you. Your soul would be damned, condemned to join him in his world and he would punish you for eternity."

Lorenzo blinked hard. He was thunderstruck. Chills went up his spine. The thought of his soul being condemned to spend eternity with a spiteful duende, scared the hell out of him.

Kan-Bah fell silent and continued to wait, looking straight ahead.

"Welcome to Jungle Cargo," Lorenzo said, intentionally changing the subject as he rose and slowly backed away from Kan-Bah.

A little while after the older American on the beach, passed in front of Jungle Cargo, Brandon saw him walking back in the opposite direction. Curious about this new person he had never seen before, here, along this fairly isolated part of the beach, but also wanting to be neighborly, Brandon, accompanied by Naja, descended the stairs leading from the deck to the front yard, and walked toward the old gentleman.

"Hello there," Brandon said, as he approached the man. The man stopped and watched as Brandon drew near. Then he looked at Naja.

"Hi there yourself," the man said. "That is a magnificent creature you have with you there. Please tell it I'm too old and dried up to taste good." He smiled as he talked.

"She's friendly," Brandon offered. "Her name is Naja, and my name is Brandon." Brandon extended his hand in friendship. The man accepted it and shook it warmly.

"I'm Don Houseman," the man said. "I bought that piece of property over there, about a thousand yards up the beach."

"You mean where the Cuyamel river comes down and empties into the sea?"

"Yep. That's the place. I'm going to build a house there. Actually, I've started construction. But I'm having trouble keeping workers."

"Why is that?"

"Well, these Hondurenos are very superstitious. Some of them said they saw a ghost, or some such. Anyway, it spooked them. So even the ones who didn't see it got scared. Now, they all abandoned ship, so to speak, went home to Sambala. I have no idea what they really saw, but it sure has thrown a monkey wrench into the works."

Brandon looked at the old gentleman. "Ghost?"

"Now wait," Don said, holding up his hand. "I know what you're thinking. But I'm just telling you what these Honduran workers have told me. I didn't say that I saw anything. I may be on a few years, but I haven't shorted out any fuses that I know of."

Brandon laughed. "Don, why don't you come on up to the house and join me for a beer? There are some people up there who I think you might enjoy meeting. You need to in any case if we're going to be neighbors."

Don nodded agreement as the two men began walking across the sandy front yard toward the stairs. "Thank you, Brandon. That would be nice. A cold beer sounds just right!"

On the deck, as Brandon and Don walked toward the patio doors, everyone in the house saw them approaching and stood to greet the newcomer.

Brandon led the way through the patio doors, and said loudly, "Look what followed me home, Mommy. Can I keep him?"

Everyone smiled, then Brandon introduced Don to everyone, including Kan-Bah.

"Don bought the property down the beach, right by the

Cuyamel delta. He's building a house there, as soon as he can get his workers to come back to work."

With that, Brandon related what Don had told him. Everyone listened intently, but no one said anything until they were certain it was alright to do so. Cold beers were produced, and the gathering was moved to the deck, where everyone gathered around the round table.

The house-girls, Anna Maria and Suyapa, brought a saucer of key lime wedges and salt. Brandon introduced the girls to the newcomer. "Don, I'd like you to meet Anna Maria and Suyapa. They work for me, keeping my life in order, which is no easy task, I assure you. But they are more than employees. They are family. I have helped raise these ladies since they were knee high."

Don rose to his feet, and said he was glad to meet the girls, shaking hands with each one of them.

That is when Brandon decided to let the cat out of the bag about the 'ghost problem,' as it came to be known. It was Brandon who opened the discussion about the green duende. The next hour was spent bringing Don Houseman up to speed. They also explained Kan-Bah's role to Don, who by this point was silent with fascination.

It was obvious by Don's reactions and remarks, plus his occasional questions that he was a very intelligent person. But he was also a very patient, compassionate and understanding person. Even Naja had no problem warming up to their new friend.

"This has got to be the most fascinating story I have ever heard," Don remarked. "And you say, this gentleman here, Mister Kan-Bah, actually plans on confronting this spirit? Is there any way I could impose myself upon your hospitality and remain here for a while this evening?"

"It's okay with us," Andrea said. "But don't you have

anybody waiting on you, back at your hotel, or wherever you're staying?"

"Oh no," Don Houseman said. "I'm alone, a widower. My wife passed a couple of years ago. As for my quarters, I have a rather nice RV set up at the property. I'm just waiting on Atlantida Power to run a line down to my place from the road. For now, when I need electricity, I just run the generator."

Brandon looked at Don. "Atlantida Power? Good luck with that. Have you made the 'proper contribution' to the gran jefe of the local office?"

"Oh dear. I thought that might come up. I guess I'd better go into town tomorrow."

"Ha! No, that won't be necessary. A rather portly gentleman…"

"Fat, chinge', asshole," Lorenzo interjected.

"Well yes, that is more accurate," Brandon admitted.

"Hijo de chingada," Lorenzo continued. "His name is Pepe Serna."

"Yes," Brandon said, looking over at Lorenzo. "Pepe Serna. He will 'arrive' at your property one day very soon to do a site inspection. You know, want to make sure where to place the pole and transformer, etc. Chances are, they will want to tap into my transformer here, and run a secondary line to your place. It would certainly make more sense than running one all the way from the main road. That would require clearing a wide path through the jungle. Lots of work, a lot of destruction to the trees around here, and cost the Atlantida a lot of money."

"Would you mind?"

"Not at all, and it wouldn't make any difference if I did. The lines belong to Atlantida Power. They can do what they want with them."

"Well, I appreciate that. So how much of a 'contribution' should I be prepared to offer this gentleman?"

Brandon looked over at Lorenzo and did the head nod.

"Depends. If you want power anytime this year, probably about a thousand limps," Lorenzo said.

"A thousand Limpiras?" Don repeated with mild surprise. "That's five hundred American Dollars."

"Yep. It's sort of 'the cost of progress' in Honduras. Where are you from, Don? I think I detect a Yankee accent."

"Pennsylvania."

"So, I was right. Forgive me for saying, but Pennsylvania is a far stretch from Honduras. What made you decide to come here? I mean, of all places...'here'?"

"Threw a dart at a map."

Everybody laughed.

"What? Are you serious?" Andrea asked.

"Serious as a heart attack," Don said. "I've missed my wife terribly since she died. Everywhere I went in our little town, something reminded me of her. I was bogging down, slowly dying inside. One night, in a dream, a voice came to me and told me to leave, to get far away from Pennsylvania. I know as sure as I am sitting here that it was Mildred's voice.

"I didn't have any idea where to go. Not one clue. So, I put a map on the wall and threw a dart at it. I promised myself, wherever that dart landed is where I would go. I was actually aiming at the United States, but gravity took hold and pulled the dart down...to Honduras. I never gave this country a moment's thought before that. So, I started reading about it in books. One day I went down and bought an RV. Here I am."

"And Cuyamel?"

"That was right in the center of where the dart struck. Actually, I looked up some satellite pictures of the area, even saw this house pretty clearly. But I couldn't figure out what all the small structures are in that compound back there."

"Parrot cages, and an old snake pit."

"Well, that solves that riddle. Okay, back to the present. So,

I need to 'make a contribution' of a thousand Limpiras to a Mister Pepe Serna to get the wheels moving on a power line to my place. Meanwhile, there seems to be the little matter of a ghost to deal with, so I can get my workers to come back. Is there anything I can do to help with this exorcism?"

"None that I know of right now, but I'm sure something will come up. Meanwhile, yes, you are most welcome to join us in our vigil, waiting for the green bastard to appear. Then, Kan-Bah is on deck."

The group's wait ended just before dark. Mosquitos had arrived with the setting of the sun and the deck was evacuated. Everyone headed inside for some air conditioning. Then, a jade green apparition appeared exactly where Lorenzo predicted it would, floating a couple of feet above the deck, just outside the patio doors. When Kan-Bah saw the apparition, he calmly rose and walked outside, through the patio doors to confront, then attempt to communicate, with the duende.

As Lorenzo, Doug, Brandon, Naja, Andrea, Don and the girls watched from the living-room, Lorenzo said nervously, "We should probably just wait here."

"Yeah," Brandon agreed. "That would be best. It would be rude to interfere."

"We wouldn't want to get in his way while he's trying to communicate with that thing," Andrea added.

"Oh no. By all means, no!" All of the group agreed emphatically, looking at one another, then back at Kan-Bah.

For the next several minutes the group watched intently as Kan-Bah appeared to try to communicate with the apparition. Then something happened that stunned, frightened and froze the observers in their spots. Kan-Bah began to morph. He started to change, and began to turn green, then join, in a small area, with the apparition. This electrically charged phenomenon lasted for several minutes. Then suddenly, the apparition faded and disappeared, leaving Kan-Bah standing alone on the deck. The Old Traveler wobbled as he turned and re-entered the house to address a stunned and silent audience.

Kan-Bah grabbed the nearest chair at the dining-room table and sagged down into it, obviously drained from his encounter. After holding his forehead in his hand for a few minutes to regain his strength, he asked for some water. Anna Maria quickly brought him a glass of cold water from the fridge.

Finally, Kan-Bah spoke. "Your unwelcome visitor is an ancient king named Spirit Sky. He is lost. He doesn't know where he is, so he doesn't know how to get back to The Lost City of The Monkey God. He says coming here was an accident. That he was looking for the descendant of Ba'alam Ma'ax, which means Jaguar Man. That descendant would be you, Don Brandon Shaw. He wound up in the stomach of a giant bird that could fly with no wings."

"The helicopter," Brandon said. "That would have to be the helicopter!"

"He tried to ask the two other humans in the bird's stomach where he was, but then the bird fell into the water and the humans perished."

"You mean he didn't intentionally murder Antonio and the helicopter pilot?"

"No. He only wanted help from them."

"Jeeeesus Christ!"

"So, were you able to find out what he wants?" Andrea asked.

"Yes. He wants two things. He wants to go home to The Lost City of The Monkey God. And then he wants the descendant of Jaguar Man to stop the humans there from violating the graves of his people."

"'The descendant of Jaguar Man'? You know, this is the second time this lollypop has come up. How can I be the long lost relative of any ancient Mayan…hot shot?"

"At this point, *how* is of little significance. That you are means everything. You are the key, and I am the translator," Kan-Bah stated.

"Well, even if I could wrap my head around this. That part about intervening is going to be tricky. He's talking about a bunch of archaeologists who are exploring the ruins," Brandon said, with a waving gesture of his arm.

"Perhaps we should take this one problem at a time," Kan-Bah said. "But now, I need a bed. Joining with the duende in his realm drained every bit of strength I have."

"Of course," Andrea said. "Whatever you need." She instructed the girls to show Kan-Bah to the guest bedroom and then make sure all of his needs were met, soap, towels, etc.

Kan-Bah was quickly installed in the biggest guest bedroom. Doug got the other one. Brandon, Andrea and Naja took the master bedroom, the housemaids, Anna Maria and Suyapa went to their room downstairs, and Lorenzo got the couch. Don wished everyone goodnight and walked back down the beach to his RV.

Exhaustion was such that supper was skipped by everyone. Sleep was at the top of the list. And this time, it was peaceful, without a duende scaring the shit out of everyone in the house. Kan-Bah had made the impossible seem almost easy.

The next morning, Anna Maria and Suyapa were up at dawn, back to their old selves, chattering like two schoolgirls, cutting fruit and boiling eggs, just like in the old days, before Brandon, Andrea and Naja had moved away to Florida. It was as if there never had been a pall over this house.

Perhaps it was the noise made by the girls, but Kan-Bah awoke and found his way to one of the showers where he spent a long time, washing. Lorenzo had no choice except to get up. He was caught in the center of the activity, but that also put him closest to the coffee pot. Within a short while, everyone was stirring and began to gather on the deck, just as in old times. This made the girls very happy and they giggled like children as they worked. But it was Lorenzo who smiled from deep inside. Having Brandon and Andrea here made him, *almost* want to thank the duende.

Kan-Bah emerged from the house, onto the deck and sought out a chair at the round metal table. Although he was his usual impassive self, he seemed pleasant enough and pleased to see the clear, bright morning emerging.

"God has provided us with a beautiful day," he said, pleasantly and matter of factly.

Brandon, Andrea, Doug, Naja and Lorenzo joined Kan-Bah at the table, taking up four of the other chairs. Naja took her place between Brandon and Andrea.

Lorenzo looked around at everyone with a slightly strange expression on his face.

"What?" Andrea asked, looking back at Lorenzo.

"No mas que, I just want to thank God for this moment. It is like the old days. You, Don Brandon, Naja, even Doug all gathered around the table for desayuno. I remember so many mornings when we were all here together, shooting the bull, planning the day. Dios mio. How I loved those days! But you know, I didn't realize how much they meant to me until all of a sudden, they weren't happening anymore. It made me realize, we take so pinche' much for granted, you know?"

Everyone managed to glance at each another in reaction to Lorenzo's words. Nothing was said in response, but everyone seated at the table felt some of what Lorenzo was talking about. Then breakfast began.

"May I join you?" A voice was heard coming from the steps. It was Don Houseman.

"Sure, neighbor!" Brandon answered. "Come have some breakfast with us."

"Thank you," Don said, as he stepped onto the deck. "I don't believe in coming empty handed to anyplace, especially at mealtime. So, I brought my own special concoction of deviled eggs." Don handed Andrea a large round tin with a lid. When she took the lid off, it revealed a couple of dozen beautifully prepared deviled eggs. She reached in without hesitation and took an egg, placed it in her mouth and began to chew.

A moment later, her eyes widened. "Oh, my word! I've never tasted deviled eggs this good. Here everyone, you have got to try these! What is this, Don? Some kind of a Pennsylvania recipe?"

"Well," Don said with a smile. "Kind of. Cooking has always been a hobby of mine. And I've always liked deviled eggs. So, I spent years perfecting them."

"Wow! To an art form, I would say," Doug managed, as he chewed on an egg.

Even the stoic Kan-Bah showed approval as he put away a few of the eggs along with other delights at the table. And so, breakfast progressed, with everybody happily eating and chatting and laughing. But, after eating for a few minutes longer, Kan-Bah turned business-like and said, "We're going to need a plan."

"Where have I heard that before?" Andrea quipped.

"See! I told you," Brandon said, as if to say, I told you so!

"Un plan?" Lorenzo asked. "Que tipo de un plan?"

Just at that moment, a large pandemonium of yellow naped amazon parrots flew over the house, being raucous, as usual. Their happy noise made it temporarily impossible for people at the table to hear one another. After the parrots passed and everyone could hear, Kan-Bah continued.

"Simply put," Kan-Bah said, as he munched on pieces of fresh mango. "We have got to figure a way to get this duende away from here and back to The Lost City of The Monkey God. That may be a simple task. Then again, it may not. Dealing with duendes is a tricky business."

Everybody looked at one another. Finally, Brandon said, "Yes. I can see how that would be a problem. You can't exactly say, 'Here, Senor Duende, have a seat next to Kan-Bah in the Jeep. Would you like a pillow, or a magazine?' So, any thoughts?"

"In fact, we might do something very similar to that," Kan-Bah said, then looked at Brandon and smiled for the very first time as he munched on fresh cut mango.

———

After breakfast, Kan-Bah went for a walk on the beach. Doug, Don, Brandon, Andrea and Lorenzo continued sitting at the table. Brandon was perplexed about what kind of a plan Kan Bah had brewing in his head and needed to get some things straight.

"Never in all my born days," he complained. "I mean, of all the problems in the world—animal protection laws, endangered species laws, disease, drug dealers…did I ever imagine that I, or you for that matter, would have to be dealing with a frigging ghost. A ghost! And not just any old ghost, but this sonofabitch wants me to intervene on it's behalf! I'm supposed to go tell a company of archaeologists that, hey, you guys are bugging the locals and you need to get out of town! And why? Because according to this guy's family tree, we're related! This is something right out of a fucking comic book, but I ain't laughing."

Doug, Don, Andrea and Lorenzo listened patiently. Brandon was up and down, sitting at the table, then pacing back and forth across the deck, looking down, mumbling under his breath.

"You know," Brandon continued, "I don't guess I ever thought very much about death. Maybe that's what's scaring me. I've been to funerals. I've seen death. I've seen people die. You remember that twisted sonofabitch voodoo priest?"

Andrea looked at Brandon knowingly. "I remember the poor Indian boy that was bitten by the fer-de-lance a lot more," Andrea said.

Suddenly Doug came alert, looking first at Andrea, then at Brandon. "Wait! Voodoo priest? You mean that crazy bastard, Smoke Jaguar, or whatever it was that he called himself? Uh, uh, what about the voodoo priest?"

"Never mind," Andrea said. "Go on, Brandon."

"I don't know. Maybe it's because I'm starting to get a little older. I just never really gave death much thought. But now, faced with this...'thing'. I mean, this cocksucker has been dead, presumably, for over a thousand years, maybe two thousand years. There's suddenly a lot of shit swirling around in my head. I was raised as a Christian. Never practiced it much. I admit that, but I've always believed. Now, here we are, faced with this fucker who has apparently been around close to two thousand years. Just a lot of unanswered questions. Never mind. They're my own demons. I'll have to deal with them."

"I've had to deal with death, on a very personal level," Don said, looking down at the deck, holding on to his walking stick. "My wife. She wanted something to make supper a little better, some spice or something. She kissed me, got in the car to go to the store. She was only supposed to be gone for five minutes. She never made it. A drunk ran a red light and killed her. I loved her with all my heart. When the cops showed up at my door to tell me about it, I thought I would die. I *wanted* to die."

"I'm so sorry," Andrea said, placing her hand on Don's shoulder.

"Thank you," Don said. "I'll see her again someday, in Heaven. Meanwhile, she wants me to live my life to the fullest that I can. That's what I have gleaned from my dreams."

"I still want to know more about the voodoo priest," Doug

said, now wide eyed, looking back and forth between Andrea and Brandon.

Andrea sighed deeply. "Brandon and I were picnicking, way up on the side of the mountain back there behind the house one day, along the Cuyamel River. Smoke Jaguar, whose real name was Reggie, snuck up on us and tried to kill us with a spear gun. Naja attacked him and killed him. It was a long time ago. It was 'un incidente de la selva'. Let's please forget it."

Doug stared at Andrea. He was now almost speechless. "'Un incidente de la selva'? Uh, uh, uh, what does that mean? 'Un incidente de la selva'? Did you report it?"

"No," Andrea admitted. "Well, no and yes. I did fill out a report to the people I was working for at the time. I let them deal with the Honduran government… or not."

Brandon was completely oblivious to the brief conversation between Doug and Andrea.

"I'll tell you something else," Brandon said, changing the subject, now gesturing toward Kan-Bah on the beach, "that strange mother fucker walking down there with sand between his toes gives me the willies. There's just something about him. He shows up in Chichicastenango out of nowhere. I mean, 'out of *nowhere*.' We hadn't told a living soul why we were there, but Kan-Bah knew. He knew everything! Not only did he know why we're there, he knew my name, he knows your name," Brandon said, looking at Andrea.

"What you talking about?" Lorenzo asked. "You mean he just showed up?"

"Yeah," Brandon said. "He just showed up… out of nowhere." Brandon then carefully told Lorenzo, Don and Doug everything that had happened since he and Andrea had gone to Guatemala. Andrea smiled at certain points of Brandon's story and interjected remarks like, "Wait till you see some of the pictures I took. Spectacular, unbelievable colors."

Brandon finally brought his catch-up story to an end with the remark, "He is just too fucking strange."

"Which part of strange are you referring to?" Andrea asked.

"I always wondered what happened to that pinche' voodoo priest," Lorenzo said with a half-smile. "So, Naja taught his ass a lesson, huh?"

"By the time Naja got through with him, I don't think he had much ass left," Andrea said.

"Ahorale!" Lorenzo said, nodding his head affirmatively. "I never did like that puto. He was an animal abuser. And I ain't got no use for animal abusers." Then he laughed, imagining the scene.

Brandon waved off the commentary about Smoke Jaguar and continued his rant about Kan-Bah. "He treats this frapping spirit like it was a next-door neighbor, or some such, that we can't get along with, has chats with the damn thing. He's done everything but sit down to tea with it. He treats the abnormal like it was… 'normal'. And that ain't normal! Come on, admit it… *he* isn't normal."

"Okay, granted," Andrea said in agreement. "But what do you care? What possible difference does that make? Right now, 'normal' is probably the last thing we need. Look, yes, the man showed up out of nowhere, but he showed up out of nowhere to *help us*. So far, it seems to me like he's doing just that. He doesn't seem to want anything except to be treated with courtesy and respect. He doesn't want money. He hasn't asked for anything except a little food, a place to sleep and to help us. So what are you freaking out about?"

"Help us. Yeah, and what about that? You don't find that at least a little bit suspicious? Everybody wants 'something'. It may not be money, but there's got to be an invoice attached to this somewhere, somehow."

"Maybe…maybe not. The man indicated he didn't want

anything."

"Andrea, everybody wants 'something'. Okay, so he doesn't want money. I'm telling you, there's got to be a price tag tied on to this somewhere. Mark my words."

"Please forgive me," Don chimed in. "I know I'm just an observer here, but I have to disagree that a price tag always has to be attached to everything. Many things are done out of friendship, or love, sometimes just respect."

"Yeah, Honey. I think you need a little more faith in your fellow man." Andrea said, looking at Brandon with pleading eyes.

They saw that Kan-Bah was walking back toward them from the beach. He climbed the steps up to the landing of the deck looking satisfied, as if he had worked out a problem in his mind.

Kan-Bah looked up at Brandon. "This entire area is resting on limestone, yes?"

"Yeah," Brandon said. "For miles in both directions. We dug a snake pit out back one time and that's what we had to carve into."

"Good!" Kan-Bah stated. "You need to have someone go back to that snake pit. It would be the perfect place to begin. You need to have them quarry a block of limestone about two meters long, a meter wide, and half that deep. When that is done, bring the block of limestone here, to this compound, and I will tell you what is needed next."

Brandon knew it would do no good to question Kan-Bah as to his motives, and it would be wasting time to try. So, he turned to Lorenzo. "Do you understand what he wants?"

Lorenzo nodded. "Si. He wants a pinche' block of limestone."

"Yes, but he's being rather specific about the dimensions. Go to Sambala and get as much manpower as you think you will need. It would help if there is anyone there who is a brick mason or stone carver, but I don't think you are gonna have much luck with that. Then get any tools you need, come back here and start 'quarrying'."

"Excuse me again," Don said, pointing his finger at the sky. "Maybe there is something I can do to help after all. You know, all my life I was a brick mason. I am going to build my new home out of limestone which we will quarry in a place right behind the house. Then, I will make the quarry hole into a swimming pool. But, the point is, I have special saws with me whose sole purpose is to cut limestone. You are welcome to use them. And for that matter, I will give you the names of my workers. Maybe you could talk to them and get them to come back if they knew they were doing something to get rid of the…'duende', did you call it?"

"Yeah, that's one of the words for it," Brandon said, a little sarcastically.

"Do they live in Sambala?" Lorenzo asked.

"Yes," Don replied, "All of them."

Don and Lorenzo had a brief conversation during which time, Don gave Lorenzo the names of his workers. Without a word, Lorenzo was on his way down the stairs, jumped into the company Jeep and left in a cloud of dust for Sambala.

Looking rather like a fifth wheel, Doug said, "You know… I could, I could help. I'm not doing anything else, just standing around."

"Fine," Brandon said. We can use all the help we can get, Appreciate it, Doug. Then Brandon turned to Kan-Bah, smiled and said, "Would you like a glass of iced tea?"

———

By late that afternoon, Don, Doug, Lorenzo and the three helpers from Sambala had a very heavy block of limestone lying across reinforced sawhorses, thanks to the special saws provided by Don. The limestone block was cut in the dimensions requested by Kan-Bah. Kan-Bah, Brandon, Don, Doug and Andrea gazed admiringly at the stone block.

Naja was a short way away, in her run, gnawing on a large piece on beef leg.

"Good job," Kan-Bah said with a smile. "Now you must start carving the stone right away, while it is still wet and soft. You don't have long to do that. First, you must carefully carve a lid and remove it. Then you must hollow out the center of the stone and make a kind of sarcophagus."

"Hot damn!" Brandon said under his breath. That's what I thought he was going to do!" Then, to Kan-Bah, "So, your plan is to talk that duende into climbing into a home-made stone coffin and taking a ride with us all the way through the Mosquitia Jungle to The Lost City of The Monkey God?"

"Yes, simple, straight forward. You are very perceptive," Kan-Bah said. "But the sarcophagus must meet very strict specifications, or the duende will reject it."

"Oh, I'm sure. What else? A picky, pain in the ass duende is what I would expect. Nothing less, of course! At this stage of the game, it doesn't take Einstein to figure it out," Brandon said, a little sarcastically. Then he walked away, shouting over his shoulder, "I need a beer. Maybe more than one beer. Anybody want to join me?"

"Oh yes," Kan-Bah said, turning. "I love cold beer."

"Yeah, me too," Andrea said. "Matter of fact, more than one is definitely in order." She hurried after Brandon.

The remainder of the afternoon was spent in the carport of the house at Cuyamel. Brandon, Andrea, Doug, Don and Kan-Bah sat around a small table drinking Salva Vida beers, the national beer of Honduras. They dosed the beers with wedges of key lime, sprinkled with salt.

But it wasn't all just about getting slightly sloshed on a hot afternoon. The beer helped Kan-Bah to open up a little and allow his companions a chance to get to know him better. As with many similar 'round table discussions', alliances were formed and more confidence in each other obtained, suspicions dispelled. In other words, the distance existing between them was eradicated. And the lubricant was Salva Vida Beer.

Three more days passed before Lorenzo and his team neared completion of their artistic task. Don had turned out to be an invaluable consultant on the project because of his vast experience in working with stone. At some point, Lorenzo had pulled up photos of other sarcophagae to use as a blueprint, such as the one from Pakal's tomb in The Temple of The Inscriptions at Palenque, in Chiapas, Mexico.

He found pictures that showed the interior of the stone coffin, and that is what he and his men used for a model. Then he encountered another problem. The photos showed, and the text revealed that the interior of the sarcophagus was painted with 'brilliant red cinnabar'. He had no idea where to get cinnabar, or if it was even possible. But without it, their experimental sarcophagus would almost certainly be a flop. All he knew was, his instructions were to adhere as closely as possible to the ancient method.

Lorenzo accepted this task as a challenge. He showed extreme interest and determination, perhaps because of his overwhelming desire to be rid of the damned duende, or maybe just because it as something of an artistic challenge. Maybe both. So, he did research, and discovered that cinnabar comes from quartz, often found near alkaline hot springs.

"Chingow! Mira, Jefe!" he exclaimed, pointing at the computer screen. "This here says that 'brilliant red cinnabar', also known as 'vermillion,' is found in quartz that comes from caves near hot springs. It's like somebody wrote the pinche' recipe just for us, because we 'just happen to have' a hot spring close to here. Jiho! We've got pinche' hot springs right up there on the side of the mountain. The only problem is, it says here that the stuff is usually found in a cave. I don't know of any cave up there. Have you ever seen a pinche' cave close to the hot spring?"

"No," Brandon admitted. "But then, I've never looked. It's pretty dense jungle up there."

Lorenzo peered at the computer screen a few moments longer. "Mira, Don Brandon. I'm going to rent some horses from next door for me and my men. We're going to go up there to that hot spring with some machetes and take a good look around, clear away some of that brush and see if there might be a cave."

Andrea, who was leaning against the back of the couch a few feet away, with her arms crossed and listening to this dialogue, said, "That's very dedicated of you, Lorenzo."

"Gracias, Doña, but it has very little to do with dedication," Lorenzo replied, as he looked at Andrea. "At least, dedication to my job, which is what I think you are talking about. This has to do with dedication to getting rid of that goddamned ghost. I want him...*it*, out of my life. And this is not a story I'm gonna tell my grandkids someday. It would probably put them in shock, and they'd wind up needing therapy. No. I just want to get rid of the chingo and try to forget this ever happened."

With that, Lorenzo stomped out the door. His body language implied, a man with a mission. He and his men rented horses from Jungle Cargo's next-door neighbor, Don Julio, and took off up the side of the mountain with digging tools, machetes, ropes and high hopes, looking for a cave containing cinnabar. He also carried a walkie talkie, since they weren't sure a cell phone would work in that remote region.

Two hours later, that walkie talkie crackled to life and a very excited Lorenzo Ponce was yelling into the microphone, "Don Brandon, Don Brandon, we found a pinche' cave. It's less than a hundred feet from that pinche' hot springs, but really hidden. We're clearing the area around the opening now with machetes."

An hour later, a slightly tired sounding Lorenzo spoke into the walkie talkie again. "Don Brandon, we've got all the undergrowth cleared from around the mouth of this cueva. We're getting ready to go in. I can't see very much with my flashlight. It looks pretty deep. Mira, I'm not too sure about this. If you don't hear from any of us within about an hour, send somebody up here to look for us, okay?"

"Of course, I will," Brandon replied. "Just take your time. Go slow and be very careful. Who knows? You might find a beautiful woman in there." Brandon chuckled.

"Yeah, right," Lorenzo answered. "If we do find one, she's bound to look better than some of those broads in Sambala. Hijole'!"

With that, the walkie talkies fell silent for a long time. Brandon began to get worried.

"Dammit!" he said. "What did I let him go up there for? He hasn't got a chance in hell of finding 'cinnabar', for God's sake. He might slip down some slope inside that cave and get killed. Who knows how big that cave is, how deep it is? He might have found another Carlsbad Caverns. Wouldn't that be something?" He looked nervously at Andrea.

Brandon went to the refrigerator and got a cold beer. He opened it, leaned against the kitchen counter, turned the bottle up, pressed it against his lips and drained it. He stood there, looking at nothing in particular, and belched. Then said, "I do some dumb things sometimes!"

Just then the walkie talkie crackled to life. "Don Brandon, Don Brandon, we've got cinnabar!" Lorenzo was yelling into the walkie talkie and laughing at the same time. "Chingow! Que bueno suerte," He was saying to the men with him. Brandon could hear them whooping with joy.

Brandon grabbed for his walkie talkie. "What?" He half shouted into the microphone.

"Si!" Lorenzo said excitedly. "We got down into the cave about a hundred feet and suddenly, we looked around, and we were surrounded by all this quartz. It was, like, all over the pinche' place. We're bringing back all we could possibly need to paint the inside of that pinche' stone coffin. I hope that goddamn duende appreciates our efforts."

"I'm not sure how he will feel, but everyone here is very grateful to you." Brandon laughed a laugh of relief. "Thank you, Lorenzo. Thank you, mi hijo, for your dedication, your determination. You've pulled off a miracle. I am so proud of you. I cannot begin to tell you how proud."

"Ah. It wasn't nothing, Jefe. Just have lots of pinche' cold beer waiting when we get back."

"Seguro que si! We will. It will be my pleasure," Brandon assured him. "You've earned it."

Brandon turned to Andrea. "He's done it! The young-un has actually done it. He's pulled off a frapping miracle. I can't believe it!" He grabbed Andrea and gave her a huge bear hug, then started dancing around the kitchen floor with her.

"The Searchers," as Lorenzo had dubbed himself and his helpers returned safely from the side of the mountain very tired, and muddy as urchins. Therefore, any thought of further work that day was out of the question. Instead, 'fiestita' was the order for the rest of the evening. Hot showers and clean clothes were at the top of the priority list, and then a break from their labors. A bit of celebration including steaks on the barbeque, lots of delicious side dishes and plenty of music from the stereo.

There was a light-hearted party mood on the deck with lots of chatter and laughter, joke telling, and in general, an attempt to forget for the moment the serious situation at hand. It was a good pressure release valve, and a good time was had by everyone including Brandon, Andrea, Don and Doug, and perhaps even Kan-Bah, who managed to shake hands with Lorenzo and his men, congratulating them on a job well done.

Even Suyapa and Anna Maria got in on the festivities, congratulating Lorenzo and joining the party.

Naja also made her presence known by doing all she could to garner attention from just about everybody. This included rubbing against their legs and doing a lot of sniffing.

It seemed to Brandon, in watching Kan-Bah out the corner of his eye, that the old man was also having a good time. He drank a few beers, talked with everyone present, smiled and seemed very much at ease. He also savored the delicious barbeque being prepared on the pit.

The distraction from worrying about the dratted ghost was sorely needed by everyone. The pressure and worry had taken its toll.

Letting off the pressure was also good for sleep. Lorenzo's helpers didn't bother returning to Sambala that night. They opted instead to sleep on pallets made of blankets on the floor of the house.

As it turned out, that was a very good thing. Rain clouds came down off the mountainside during the night and brought rain that made soft pattering sounds on the roof. That made sleep even deeper, better, more healing, more restful. Naja, asleep at the foot of Brandon's bed, also slept a deep, peaceful rest.

Genuine rest was long overdue, and something the duende had inadvertently robbed them of. But thanks to the intervention of Kan-Bah, they seemed to be on the trail of a solution. Not a simple one, perhaps, or an easy solution, but a solution, never-the-less.

Dawn found Kan-Bah standing alone on the deck, looking out at the sleepy Caribbean. Small, lazy waves washed up on the beach in front of Jungle Cargo as the girls busied themselves with breakfast, giggling and chattering like always. The day was emerging.

Lorenzo and his helpers appeared one by one on the deck with coffee cups in hand and looking like parrots had been making nests in their hair.

"Chingow!" Lorenzo said. "What was in that rum last night? Sabes que, I used to get on Don Brandon's ass for drinking too much. Now, I need to have a talk with myself! Hijole'!" He sat in a lounge chair and held his head in his hands.

Kan-Bah left his viewing spot, against the deck railing and walked over to Lorenzo. "Your work is very important. Nothing should distract you from completing it as quickly as possible."

Then Kan-Bah opened his left hand as widely as he could and placed it against the top of Lorenzo's head. Lorenzo was frozen and did not move for the next thirty seconds. When Kan-Bah took his hand away, Lorenzo looked up wide eyed at the old Mayan in disbelief.

"Thank you!" Lorenzo managed to say.

Then, without a word, Kan-Bah went to the other three men who were Lorenzo's helpers and repeated his hand-on-head ceremony with them. They too were in shock because when Kan-Bah removed his hand, their hangover pain had completely disappeared.

"Now," Kan-Bah said. "Eat a good desayuno. You need your strength. Then continue your work."

Lorenzo walked over and whispered to Andrea, "I repeat, who the fuck is this guy?"

"Kan-Bah," She answered matter of factly.

"I don't mean that," Lorenzo whispered with a hiss. "Goddammit, I know his name. What I mean is, *who* is he? You know what I'm asking."

"I wouldn't know any more than you do," Andrea answered honestly. "How's your head?"

"My cruda is completely gone. Completely! That mother has some kind of pinche' magic, and he just scares the shit out of me."

"He's got something, that's for sure," Andrea said as she looked in the direction Kan-Bah had taken, down the stairs, apparently to inspect the sarcophagus under construction.

"Tell me, Lorenzo. What he did for you. Was it good, or bad?"

"Well, good, of course. He took my pain away. But…"

"Stop right there," Andrea said. "Everything we have seen him do is good in one way or another. Right?"

Lorenzo was speechless. He just looked at Andrea. She repeated her question. "Right?"

Lorenzo still couldn't speak. He simply nodded his head yes. Lorenzo skipped breakfast. He was too shook up from the 'hand on head' healing that Kan-Bah had just performed. Instead, he led his three men, who were equally stunned, down the stairs to locate the cave quartz and start grinding it into a fine powder to make an ancient form of paint that just might impersonate the old, brilliant red cinnabar which was required.

By early afternoon, the four men's efforts were paying off. The quartz had been ground into a fine, chalk-like powder. With the measured addition of the proper amount of water, they had cinnebar paint and began to brush it onto the interior walls of their limestone creation.

By now, Don Houseman had joined them to see if there was any way he could contribute to the project. He had been mostly just an observer, but he was rapidly becoming a welcome and trusted friend. It was so obvious that Don Houseman was a man with a good and loving heart.

However, in observing him, although she tried to be subtle about it, Andrea saw a sadness about Don Houseman, and perhaps a loneliness. It was a little poignant, she thought, and wished the man could be happier. Life had not been kind to this old gentleman in taking away from him the thing he loved the most in life. But despite whatever he was feeling inside, he was a gentleman, and showed all the earmarks of being a devoted friend and an all-around good person.

As the Jungle Cargo contingent looked on, Kan-Bah carefully inspected the stone coffin and gave it his blessing, nodding his head appreciatively. The pseudo sarcophagus was ready. But now they had to deal with the problem of how to transport it. It weighed several hundred pounds—far too heavy for the Jeep. There was no choice. The old company flat-bed truck would have to be brought into service as the hearse for the portable crypt. Lorenzo backed the truck up as close as possible to the stone coffin, and all seven men struggled to slide it on board. Once there, it was covered with a blue plastic tarp and tied down tightly with rachet straps. At long last, it was ready to go.

All preparations were made for a semi-long trip into the Mosquitia. Vehicles were topped off with gas, suitcases were packed. Lorenzo drove the girls to La Ceiba to go grocery shopping so they could move back into the house permanently and have plenty of food stocked up while everyone was gone. Besides, Doug Bennet would be with them, so they had to take that into account. Then Andrea had a talk with them to let them know the duende was leaving and would not be back. They had nothing more to be afraid of. This helped greatly to dispel their fear.

All preparations were made. Now all they had to do was wait for the temperamental duende to decide to make an appearance.

That happened at about midnight. The light emanating from the ghost woke Kan-Bah, who had been dozing on the sofa. He hadn't gone to bed because he had been hoping for this moment. He immediately approached the duende.

In ancient Mayan Pech, he somehow got across to the ghost that if he wanted to go home, the people here would help him. They had even prepared a vehicle for him to travel safely in. All he had to do was trust them, and get in the sarcophagus, then stay there until he was called forth by Kan-Bah.

Amazingly, it worked. The astray spirit wanted nothing more than to return to The Lost City of The Monkey God. He would cooperate. He followed Kan-Bah down the steps to the truck, floating a few feet above the ground, and when Kan-Bah spoke, then gestured toward the sarcophagus on the back of the truck, the glowing spirit seemed to meld into it and disappeared. Kan-Bah returned to the deck with a satisfied expression on his face.

"Our duende is ready for his journey," Kan-Bah said triumphantly.

"Well done," Brandon offered.

At dawn, the two-vehicle convoy set out from Jungle Cargo. As in a time past, Brandon and Andrea drove the Jeep with Naja sprawled out across the back seat. Lorenzo, with Kan-Bah as his passenger, drove the old blue truck. The duende, presumably, was safely ensconced in the sarcophagus.

Doug had happily volunteered to stay behind and try to restore normalcy to Jungle Cargo. He had no desire to make the trip into the Mosquitia Jungle. Hearing about it was as close as he wanted to get. And now he would have good company in the form of Don Houseman to talk with, play checkers with, or commiserate with.

As the two vehicles pulled out of the driveway, all travelers waving at Doug, Don and the girls as they left, Brandon said to Andrea, "Nobody would believe why we are making this trip....*Nobody!*"

Andrea laughed and settled in for the long, bumpy ride.

CHAPTER FOUR

Return to the Jungle Inn

THE CONVOY HAD BARELY PASSED BALFATE BEFORE THE SKIES ON their right side started to look ugly and turn dark blue. Lightning could be seen playing in the clouds, accompanied by the distant sound of thunder. Brandon eyed the ominous scene but said nothing. He didn't need to. Andrea knew exactly what he was thinking. A deluge along this jungle road is exactly what they did not need. It would turn the whole thing into one endless mud-pie. They weren't so worried about the Jeep getting stuck as the old blue truck that seemed to struggle even under the best of circumstances.

Brandon picked up his walkie talkie and pressed the talk button. "Lorenzo, you guys alright back there?"

"We're fine," came the response. "I just hope we can get as much of this road behind us as possible before the pinche' bottom drops out."

"I'll vote for that," Brandon said.

But the rain did come, slowly at first, then heavier and heavier. The worry was that at the bottom of each hill, where the water would accumulate, this excuse for a dirt road which was in reality only a bulldozed trail through the jungle, would start to turn into a muddy nightmare. Luckily, it had been a pretty dry season, so the soil soaked up a lot of the water, at least for a while.

Brandon once again picked up the walkie talkie to speak with Lorenzo. "We're close to Trujillo. I hadn't wanted to stop there. But we're gonna have to get these vehicles off of this road and see if there's a chance of waiting this out."

"Sad Mary's?" Lorenzo asked.

"Yeah, where else, goddammit," Brandon said with resignation. "Sad Mary's."

"Heaven help us!" Andrea said, as she held onto the passenger brace. She had only been to Sad Mary's Café once in her life, but that had been enough to last her a lifetime.

Within a few miles, Brandon spotted the small sign that said "TRUJILLO" with an arrow pointing to the left. The convoy turned in the direction of the arrow, and within a couple of minutes approached a concrete road. They were safe from sinking into the mud, at least for now.

Three miles farther on and Brandon pulled over to the curb in front of a whitewashed, cinderblock building. It was hard to see the sign on the front of the building through the heavy rain, but it didn't matter. They all knew they were at Sad Mary's Café.

Everyone that is except for Kan-Bah, and he could have cared less. He was on his own journey, in his own world, which seemed to be apart from everyone else.

Thunder rolled as the travelers got out of their vehicles and dashed for the front door of Sad Mary's Café. The front door was nothing but a screen door, so light and the smells of cooking spilled from inside.

The minute they entered the café, Sad Mary greeted them in her own unique way. "Well, kiss my wrinkled up old ass! Look who we've got here. Brandon Shaw, and his jaguar, his lady, Lorenzo, and I don't recognize this sour puss looking fucker here." Sad Mary stuck out her hand, "Hi there. I'm Mary."

Kan-Bah accepted her gesture of friendship, although Maya Indians do not shake hands in the same traditional sense that most people do. They just touch the palm of the person's hand they are greeting, and quickly withdraw their hand.

"This fucking rain is something else, huh?" Mary said, looking out the screen door. "Marta," she called to the worker in the kitchen, "Bring these people some hot coffee, lots of it."

Turning her attention to Brandon and Andrea, she said, "What in the hell brings you out in this crazy weather? You been down here long enough, I thought you had better sense."

"We're on our way into the Mosquitia," Brandon said truthfully.

"The Mosquitia?" Mary repeated. "Is they another snake migration going on?"

"Not that I know of," Brandon replied. "We're on a mission of a different kind."

Mary eyed Brandon suspiciously. "Uh huh. Well. Y'all want breakfast? Or do you think some of my yuca and pork stew might wake you up better?

"Looks like we've got some time to kill," Brandon said. "I don't know about anybody else, but I'd like some fried eggs with a side of platanos."

Mary called her guest's wishes out to Marta in the kitchen. A voice responded from that area. "Si. Muy pronto, Senora."

Everyone found seats at various tables. Brandon looked at Mary, who seemed older than the last time he had seen her. She looked more tired, somehow.

"So, how have you been, Mary?"

Mary sank down into a chair next to Brandon and Andrea. "Ah, it's the same old shit, day after day, after goddamn fucking day. I wake up and can't even figure out why I bother. Then I come down to this stinking shithole to cook up slop for a bunch of un-appreciating half breed bastards that sit around and pick their noses when they eat. I'll tell you, Brandon, I've reached the point in life where I'm asking why.

"I fucked myself a lot of years ago when I fell in love with a prick who used me like a cheap whore and then dumped me when it became too 'inconvenient' to come see me. You know what? I was a fairly good-looking woman at one point in my life. Then I let my heartbreak take me down a bad road of no return." Sad Mary looked up as if she had thought of something. "Wait a second. I want to show you something."

She rose from her chair and walked to the back of the café where she opened a drawer and withdrew an old, framed 8" x 10" black and white photo. She returned to the table, carrying the photo as if it were a treasure. Indeed, it was.

"Take a look at this," she said reverently. "This was me forty years ago."

Brandon gazed at the photograph and could not believe his eyes. He had heard that Sad Mary had been attractive in her day, but that had been an understatement. The woman in the picture was beautiful, well dressed and looked dignified, refined. Brandon had trouble believing this was the same old hag that stood before him in a soiled apron. He passed the picture across the table so Andrea could see it. When she focused on the photo, her eyes bulged. Mouth agape, she looked from the photo, to Sad Mary.

"Mary…" Andrea managed. "I don't know what to say. You were a beautiful woman."

"Yeah, but not anymore," Sad Mary added. "I let my hope die because of heartbreak. I should have never done that. I turned myself from the beauty in this picture into the wrinkle-bucket you see before you today. I did it. Me. I did it to myself. You know, I never loved but once. Oh, I had other chances. Should have took 'em. I didn't because I was a one-man woman. Guess I still am, not that it makes any difference anymore. Who the fuck would want a worn out, over the hill, rusty old bucket like me? Time fucks us more than anything else in the world. There ain't no second chances, not at anything, and especially anything good."

Mary looked up at Brandon, then Andrea. She stared Andrea straight in the eye. "Take a damn good look at me. Lemme tell you something, I hope the very best for you and this jungle man here. But if, God forbid, something goes wrong and you find yourself with empty arms, don't waste a fucking minute of your life, sitting around, crying over spilt milk. Life's too short and they ain't no second chances. You hear me? Time will fuck you in the ass without ever blinking. One day, you look young, like you do right now. The next day, time has robbed you of everything, your youth most of all."

By now, Sad Mary's voice was quavering. "Get away from this fucker and find yourself another before you can spit, and it hits the ground. I'm tellin' you gospel. Take it to your heart, pretty girl. Don't throw away the life that the good Lord done give you. You don't even have to die to go to hell for that. One look at me is all the proof you need that I'm telling you the truth. I wasted my life. I wasted my whole fucking life!"

Then she looked at Brandon. "Sorry, big boy. I don't mean no disrespect. I really don't. I would just hate to see what happened to me, happen to her."

After that, Sad Mary quit talking for a while. She put her face in her hands and sobbed softly. Andrea went to her and held her.

The rain continued to fall in heavy sheets, accompanied by rolling thunder. Sad Mary's sorrow was gracefully hidden among the sounds of the thunder.

Two hours later, after having eaten a sumptuous breakfast prepared by Marta, the group was still at the small cafe. Brandon stood at the screen door, looking out at the rain. Naja sat faithfully beside him. Everyone else relaxed at tables, drinking soft drinks.

"We just do not need this," Brandon said more to himself than anyone else. "All I want to do is get this trip... this 'mission' over with. Where the hell is the rain coming from anyway? It's not the rainy season, is it?"

"The more jungle they cut down, the more it affects the weather," Lorenzo said. "It's like nature is trying to fight back."

Andrea stared blankly into space, thinking about something known only to her, perhaps the scene that had unfolded earlier with Sad Mary had touched her.

Rolling thunder started far away, then traveled down from the mountains until it crossed over the town of Trujillo and continued out to sea.

Kan-Bah sat, stoic, uncomplaining, as if tomorrow and yesterday were the same. He contented himself with sipping coffee and eating small bites of home-made pan dulce. Anyone looking at him would think that he could see into the future and knew the outcome of this safari.

An hour more and the rain started to let up. When it did, customers started showing up at Sad Mary's, wanting a late lunch. But when they saw Naja, most of them quickly left, some without editorial comment, but most with an expletive. One or two people were brave enough to enter, seeing the jaguar and being more curious than frightened.

Is it a male, or female?" one young man asked.

"Female," Brandon answered.

"She is beautiful," the young man said enthusiastically. "May I pet her"

"I think so," Brandon answered. "Just approach her slowly. "Her name is Naja."

The young man squatted down and extended his hand for Naja to smell. He crooned her name softly, then reached behind her ears and scratched gently.

"This is amazing!" he said. "I'm touching this beautiful animal, a real jaguar."

The young man spent the next few minutes petting Naja, then withdrew with a huge smile on his face. "Thank you," he said to Brandon.

Brandon nodded with a smile. After that, he decided to pull the plug. He thanked Sad Mary warmly, hugged her, then placed some Limpiras in her hand and led the way outside, back to the vehicles. However, even as he started the Jeep, he felt apprehensive and sat with the motor idling for several long moments before putting the vehicle in gear and pulling away from the curb.

He had traveled Honduran roads after heavy rain and seen what always managed to happen. Some overloaded truck always, *always* got stuck at the bottom of a hill where water accumulated. Then, if any other traffic wanted to continue along the road, they had to try and negotiate a way around the stuck vehicle without also getting stuck. It was a fool's game.

On this day, however, providence was looking out for Brandon Shaw and Company. Despite the heavy rains, the roads were reasonably firm and other traffic was almost non-existent. Except for a few road-side villages, there just wasn't that much population to the east of Trujillo, and that dwindled even more the closer one drew to the Mosquitia Jungle.

It feels like the end of the world there, or perhaps the beginning of it. Human habitations are replaced by animal life and instead of seeing an occasional Indian walking beside the road, it is no surprise to spot tropical wildlife including Central American crocodiles, very large snakes including boa constrictors or the deadly fer-de-lance.

Even an occasional tapir has been spotted, ocelots, coati-mundis, and of course monkeys everywhere, howler monkeys, spider monkeys, white fronted capuchin monkeys. There are also thousands of parrots and macaws, some flying overhead, others perched in trees near the road, watching the convoy pass.

In some places, there were clear meadows covered with bright green grass, and inevitably in those meadows, there would be a gigantic kapok tree, as big as a house at the base with roots reaching outward above the ground like giant talons. The trees, also known as 'ceiba' trees, reach heights of over two hundred feet with slick trunks nearly to the top where branches spread out and are consistently covered with orchids and bromeliads.

Parrots love to perch in these lofty branches and frequently build nests there. The view is no doubt spectacular and unobstructed, so the birds feel safe.

By the time the convoy reached the edge of the Mosquitia Jungle, they had left all signs of civilization far behind, and it was a very vulnerable feeling. If something happened here, there was absolutely no one to turn to for help. You were on your own, and it tended to make one look closely before they stepped anywhere.

That feeling would grow distinctly more profound the moment they entered the darkness of the Mosquitia. Perhaps because of this, the travelers decided to stop for a minute and disembark the vehicles to walk around.

Andrea was shocked when she looked at the Jeep and the truck. Both were entirely covered in mud and almost unrecognizable. "These things are going to need a wash job...*bad!*" she said.

Brandon said nothing, just laughed. But worry played across his face and in his eyes. He wasn't looking forward to the next few hours. After a few minutes, he decided the group could delay no longer.

"Saddle up!" he said. And everyone climbed back into their respective vehicles. Motors roared to life, and the safari continued slowly ahead, into the dark hell. The jungle growth was so thick here they felt like they were in a tunnel, a dark tunnel, for the vegetation blocked most of the light.

The progress ahead was slowed to a crawl because of millions of surface roots which, although they formed a hammock-like support which kept vehicles from sinking into the mud, they also made for an extremely bumpy ride. Both vehicles crawled across this wooden spider's web in low gear; the side rails on the blue truck clattering loudly as they rocked back and forth.

Andrea held on for dear life, remembering her previous trip here. And though she refused to complain, she felt like her stomach was doing flip flops. Naja was having a rough time in the back seat trying to maintain balance, even with four legs, and lying prone on the seat. Brandon's jaw was clenched. Although he had been here and endured this a few times previously, each time seemed like the first time. There simply was no such thing as 'getting used to it.'

Three torturous hours passed before the dark tunnel gave way and they arrived at the miracle oasis in the Jungle known as, Didier Marin's *JUNGLE INN*. Here, the jungle had been cleared away a hundred yards or more in front of the freshly painted, white, cinder-block building.

The Jungle Inn was truly a miracle; really! An aerial view would show the main building of The Jungle Inn as something of a 'T' shape with a straight line running a hundred yards by fifty feet wide. In the center of this hundred yard 'T' was a grand entrada, tiled with a broad cement staircase. The open breezeway, tiled with royal blue Spanish tile, led straight through the facility to a broad restaurant on the right side, and a bar on the left. Behind the hotel was a garden with carefully tended flowers and bushes that brought a kind of civility to this untamed kingdom in the middle of the Mosquitia Jungle.

To the left and right sides of the main entrance area were the wings that formed the bar of the 'T', where there were well appointed rooms, twenty on each side, with a corridor running between them. Sconces along the walls pleasantly lit the corridor and made visitors feel safe in a place where 'safe' was not a throw-away phrase.

Standing at the top of the four-foot-high landing, wearing his tropical guayavera shirt and beige trousers was the giant heart of a man, a very short person in stature, and a leper named Didier Marin. As everyone pulled up in front of the hotel and got out of their vehicles, Didier greeted them warmly, spread his arms wide and said,

"Oh my! Welcome back, Brandon, Andrea, Lorenzo." Then, turning to Kan-Bah he said, "And who is this new friend that I haven't met yet?"

Brandon said, "Didier, this is Kan-Bah."

Didier shook hands with Kan-Bah and said, "So very glad to meet you. Welcome to my house. We are most honored to have a spirit walker visit us."

Then Didier said to everyone, "You must be exhausted. Please come into the bar for refreshments, on the house of course. Andrea, as I remember it, you rather like our special jungle juice."

"Sounds heavenly, Didier," Andrea said.

"And by the way," Didier said with a huge smile, "Merry Christmas to you all! Your rooms are all ready for you."

"Oh, my goodness! Merry Christmas to you too. And of course, you knew we were coming?" Brandon said with a smile.

"There are no secrets in the jungle," Didier said to Brandon, with a knowing smile. "Well, actually, there are many secrets hidden within the darkness of the jungle. But no secrets from me."

As they walked into the restaurant/bar area, Andrea was shocked to see an eight foot tall, beautifully decorated, Christmas tree, complete with a white cotton apron surrounding it's base and carefully wrapped gifts stacked beneath the tree. Hundreds of gaily colored lights twinkled, making the holiday display spectacular.

Andrea was brought to a halt in her tracks, her mouth open with awe and joy. "Didier! You have a Christmas tree! A beautiful Christmas tree!"

"Thank you," Didier said. "Of course, we don't have any conifers here in the jungle, so I'm afraid that beautiful fir tree comes in a box. But the decorating is all added and done by hand, with a great deal of patience and referencing of photographs."

"It looks just beautiful. You've done a spectacular job. Oh my! I am so impressed. It is so beautiful. And so unexpected!"

"Thank you, Andrea. I hope it brings you a little joy in this glorious season."

Andrea bent down and gave the little man a warm hug.

Kan-Bah asked where his room was. The long trip had taken its toll on him. Didier had a bell-boy show him the way. Kan-Bah slowly shuffled his way along the corridor, following the bell-boy.

Then Didier turned his attention to Naja with genuine affection. He stroked her head and scratched her behind the ears. "Guess what Didier has for Naja? I've got a big tapir leg waiting here just for you, and another surprise, we have a new horse trough filled with water, just for you to play in! Yes. Uncle Didier had it imported just for Naja."

He then led Naja to a special area set up just for her outside the tiled bar/restaurant area, in the garden. Once in the garden, Didier then asked the cook to fetch the tapir leg from the cooler. Naja accepted the gift and begin gnawing. She was very content.

When Didier rejoined Brandon and his group, Brandon said, "Thank you, Didier. You're a good person and I know that Naja loves coming here."

"Oh, my pleasure. I admire Naja a great deal and I am always thrilled to see her."

Brandon then leaned over and said to Didier very softly, "What did you mean, 'spirit walker'?"

Didier looked a little surprised. "You mean, you didn't know?"

"Know what? That we've got a 'very unusual' person with us. Yeah, I knew that. And… Well, I've seen him do some pretty strange things. Actually, I've seen him do some very strange things. I've just never heard the phrase, 'spirit walker'. What exactly is a spirit walker?"

"Well, some say they are actually spirits who take on human form when they want to walk among people. I guess you could best describe them as the Mayan version of an angel. Spirit walkers always appear to do good for people."

"That's good news!" Brandon said. "But how did you know?"

"I saw it in his eyes," Didier said with a smile.

"Saw it in his eyes? Saw it in his eyes? I've looked in his eyes. All I saw was eyes!"

"You have to learn how to look deeper, Brandon Shaw. Remember what Shakespeare said: 'There are more things in heaven and on earth, Horatio, than are dreamt of in your philosophy.'"

Everyone chuckled at that and were beginning to relax from the long, arduous trip when suddenly a tall, angular man, who needed a shave and a bath, sitting at the bar and apparently a little bit drunk snarled, "Is this a hotel or a goddamned zoo? I gotta tell you, I'm not having a good time, sitting here listening to that piss-ant panther, or whatever it is, crunch bones."

Brandon spoke loud enough for the man to hear. "Sorry she's bothering you, Mister. But it's been a long trip and she's hungry. She's got to eat."

"Well, let her eat someplace else," the drunk said. "This is supposed to be a restaurant for people, not wild animals."

Didier stood up. "This is my hotel, sir. And my restaurant. I will have whoever I want here. Now I would advise you to put a lid on it, sir."

The drunk got off of his stool and came toward Didier, who had been sitting with Brandon. "Fuck you, Shorty. Nobody tells me to put a lid on it."

It was at that moment that Brandon rose from his chair, and when the drunk was within striking range, Brandon unleashed one, striking the drunk smack in the middle of his face. The sound of cartilage breaking resounded throughout the restaurant/bar as the drunk staggered backwards, fell and hit the floor. He was out cold. Blood flowed from his nose.

Didier had Pedro, the bartender, bring a pitcher of water, which Didier poured over the man's face. When the drunk started to wake up, Didier said to him, "Here's the way it's going to be. You're going back to your room tonight and try to sober up. In the morning, you're leaving here, and I don't ever want to see you around here again."

Didier then turned to Pedro and said, "Help this idiot to his room. He is no longer a guest here and he is to be served nothing. No food, and certainly no drink. Loan him a first aid kit so he can quit bleeding all over everything."

"Si, Senor," Pedro responded, then bent down to take hold of the drunk's arm.

Brandon helped Pedro pull the man to his feet and pointed him in the direction of his room. The drunk staggered away, holding his face with one hand. That, they thought, was the end of that. They made a couple of uncomplimentary comments, then turned their conversation back to what it had been before the ruckus. Pedro brought some rags and started cleaning up the blood and water.

But a few minutes later, the drunk reappeared. Only, this

time he was armed with a large caliber revolver, which he aimed at Naja and started firing as he walked toward her. The multiple reports were thunderous.

The frightened jaguar bolted and disappeared into the nearby underbrush. Meanwhile, Brandon was on his feet in a flash, sprinted across the room like a lightning bolt and pushed the drunk as hard as he could. The drunk went sprawling pell-mell headlong forward and dropped the pistol as he slid across the floor.

Brandon didn't wait for him to get up. He rushed the man and began kicking him in the ribs repeatedly and with all the force he could muster. When his attack began to abate, he grabbed the unconscious man by the ankle and dragged him through the breezeway to the front landing of the hotel, down the steps and into the parking lot. That is where he left him, still unconscious.

"Merry Christmas, you crazy bastard!" Brandon spat through clenched teeth.

Without another word, Brandon returned to where the drunk had dropped the pistol and collected it. He checked to see how many bullets were left in the cylinder, then emptied it, putting the bullets in his pocket.

Andrea, remembering a time long ago on the beach in front of Jungle Cargo, said advisedly, "Don't kill him, Brandon. We don't need that kind of trouble."

"Let's go find Naja," Brandon said.

For the next several hours, Brandon, Lorenzo, Andrea and Didier searched for the terrified cat. They called her name repeatedly and scoured the foliage around the Jungle Inn, but she did not respond. There wasn't a sign of her, and Brandon became increasingly frightened that one of the drunk's bullets had found it's mark, that his precious jaguar was lying dead somewhere close by. Brandon was beside himself with anguish and fury.

"If she's dead, so is he," Brandon said. Tears of fear and rage found their way down his cheeks which he constantly wiped away with the back of his hand. All through the night, he could be heard walking through the undergrowth, calling her name. "Naja! Naja!"

At one point, he returned to the hotel parking lot to confront the drunk. By now the man had regained consciousness but was still sitting in the same spot where Brandon had left him, clutching at his broken ribs and breathing shallow because of the pain when he tried to inhale.

Brandon cocked the hammer on the revolver and pointed it at the man's head. "If we find that any of your bullets hit Naja, I'm going to kill you, you miserable sack of shit, mother fucking bastard," Brandon said matter of factly.

"I need a doctor," the drunk whined.

"Yeah? Too bad. Ain't no doctor out here. You should have thought about that before you acted like an ass-hole," Brandon answered.

"I'm hurt," the drunk said. "You broke my ribs."

"I repeat, you should have thought of that before you did something so goddamn stupid," Brandon said. "Count your blessings that I didn't break your neck. It's what you deserve. Naja wasn't hurting you. All she wanted was to eat her supper in peace. She was hungry. Don't you have any compassion for animals?"

By now, the other members of Brandon's party had gathered on the landing, and stood there, watching. Brandon raised his arm and pointed his palm at the group, instructing them to not come down from the landing.

"Listen to me, you piss-ant," Brandon snarled. "You've got one chance and only *one* chance to live. Get your worthless ass up and start walking."

"To where?" the drunk asked, looking around into the dark night. "We're in the middle of the jungle!"

"You noticed that, did you? You wanted to act like an animal, I'm going to give you a chance to live like one. I'm going to count to ten. If I can still see you at the end of that count, I'm going to blow your brains all over the parking lot. One... Two..."

Frightened out of his wits because he knew the large man looming before him was serious, the drunk struggled to his feet and limped away, bent over in pain, into the darkness.

Andrea said, "Brandon, he'll die out there."

"Most likely," Brandon said, and ascended the steps of the landing, still holding the pistol.

"Who is that guy?" Brandon asked Didier.

"Well, he *was* one of the people doing research at the archaeological site."

"Archaeological site? You mean The Lost City of The Monkey God? Is that now being referred to only as 'The archaeological site'?"

"That, and 'The Lost City'," Didier said.

The small group clustered there on the landing of the hotel. Brandon peered into the darkness with worry on his face. "I've got to find Naja. She may be hurt."

Andrea could feel Brandon's pain and came to him, wrapping his arm in her hands. But he was inconsolable.

For the next three days, rains came to the jungle. But that didn't stop Brandon's search. He wandered the forest on foot and sometimes in the Jeep, searching, calling, looking in every dark spot hoping against hope that he would not find Naja, as he feared he would, injured, or worse. He searched non-stop. He did not sleep, but rather, sank deeper into anguish with each passing hour as he scoured every possibility in the jungle.

Exhausted and half drowned, he returned to the hotel where Andrea anxiously awaited him. She quickly ushered him into a hot shower and made him stay there. After removing his rain-soaked clothes and scrubbing him clean, she led him to the bed and tucked him between clean sheets where he quickly fell into a deep, exhausted sleep.

When at last he awoke, the rain had stopped. Brandon, still groggy from exhaustion, sat on the side of the bed for a long while before trying to climb into clothes and go down the corridor to the restaurant.

Upon arrival, he found his small group, including Kan-Bah, sitting together at a round table, close to the Christmas tree, sipping something cool to fight off the heat and stifling humidity. When they saw him coming, they greeted him warmly. Didier motioned to Pedro to bring Brandon one of the refreshing fruit drinks.

Andrea reached out to touch Brandon's arm. "How are you, honey?" she inquired.

Brandon nodded his head. "Okay, I guess. Any sign of Naja?"

Andrea nodded her head and said no. Everyone else shook their head in concert.

This morning, there was a new person at the Jungle Inn, not sitting at the bar, but rather at a table finishing breakfast. He overheard the conversation going on at Brandon's table.

"Excuse me," the stranger said. "Is somebody missing?"

"Brandon's jaguar," Didier replied. "We had an incident here a few nights ago. A drunk visitor at the hotel took a shot at her with a pistol and scared her. She ran off into the bush. We haven't seen her since."

"Oh, my God!" the stranger said. "I am so sorry to hear that. Uh, my name is Bruce, Bruce Burns." He extended his hand in greeting to everybody. "I'm sorry we're meeting under such stressful circumstances."

"Yes, I know," Didier said, shaking the man's hand. "I am Didier. This is my little store here."

"And an amazing 'little store' it is, Didier. Just absolutely amazing. I must ask you about it, but later."

After introductions were made, Bruce Burns asked, "May I join you?" indicating an empty chair.

"Certainly," Didier said.

"I don't mean to butt in, but I may be able to help."

Brandon looked at the newcomer. "How?" he asked.

"Well," Bruce Burns began, "I am a researcher. I was hired to do an aerial map of The Lost City of The Monkey God."

"How are you going to do that?" Brandon asked.

"I've already done it, with a drone."

"A drone?"

"Yes," Bruce said. "I'm a licensed drone pilot. I mapped and photographed every square inch of the Lost City. It's a very sophisticated drone. If you would like, I could fly low, over the jungle canopy. We could program the drone to search overlapping grids and show every blessed thing out there within a mile or so, or even farther than that if it becomes necessary."

Bruce immediately had the group's attention. "That's amazing!" Brandon said excitedly. "We would pay you."

"Oh, no. I wouldn't want money. My reward would be, helping you get your jaguar back. It's obvious that you love her very much. I'll be right back. There's no time to waste."

Without ceremony, Bruce Burns left to walk toward the front of the hotel where his vehicle was parked. He returned shortly with a large, aluminum box resembling a suitcase. He laid it on an empty table, opened it and withdrew a strange looking flying machine with six horizontal propellers.

"This is Snoopy!" he said proudly. "Obviously named in reverence of the world's most famous beagle, but also because with the high-resolution camera on this baby, we can search that twisted mass of limbs and vines out there without missing so much as a garden snail or a tree frog. I'll fly low and slow, at about three hundred feet up, the camera will be looking straight down with a special attachment that is heat sensitive.

Anything with a body temperature of more than ninety degrees will show up on the screen like a light bulb."

Everyone listening to Bruce Burns was speechless. He then reached into the metal box and withdrew a controller and a large electronic tablet that operated off of satellites, the only way he could record this far away in the jungle.

"Shall we retire to the patio?" Bruce said with a smile, walking out to the patio area behind the hotel. As he set everything up, he also asked that his charger be plugged in somewhere.

"We'll have to change batteries about every forty minutes," he explained.

After all preparations were made, Bruce launched his aircraft. The drone went straight up, very quickly. The search was officially on. At Bruce's instruction, everyone turned their attention to the full color monitor. Having never seen a drone in action before, they were in awe at what they saw on the vivid, full color screen. They could see the hotel and jungle from a vantage point here-to-fore impossible except by helicopter. And even that did not compare to this view which was almost microscopic.

Bruce pressed a few more buttons and grid lines appeared on the screen. He inputted instructions into the mini-computer regarding a 'search pattern', and the drone flew away as if it had a mind of its own.

For the next two hours, Snoopy see-sawed back and forth across the jungle canopy, spotting thousands of monkeys and birds, a couple of ocelots, coati mundi, kinkachoos, a tapir or two, and a myriad of other creatures.

Bruce had to bring Snoopy in for a landing about every half hour to change batteries. Then, it was back into the air, resuming the search where the drone had left off.

Suddenly, Bruce saw something and backed Snoopy up several feet with the controller. "There!" he exclaimed there are two large cats. Looks like a black one and a regular jaguar with rosettes. Let me zoom in tighter."

Bruce put Snoopy in hover mode and zoomed in on the two cats. Brandon stared intently at the screen.

Suddenly, Brandon proclaimed, "By God! That's Naja! She's alive!" He tried to rise from his chair, but his relief was such that he was weakened. Tears came to his eyes and blurred his vision. He quickly wiped them away. His chest was heaving as he gasped for breath. "Naja is alive!" he proclaimed. More tears of joy found their way down his cheeks. At the same time, a general cheer went up from everyone.

"Where is that?" Brandon wanted to know. "Where are we looking?"

Bruce did some quick calculations. "About two miles north-east of here."

At that very moment, Naja and her new friend both heard Snoopy and looked up to see what it was. Brandon was watching. "That *is* her, for sure! There is no doubt. There is nooo doubt!"

Brandon grabbed Bruce and gave him a bear hug. "I am forever in your debt," Brandon said. Then he, Andrea and Lorenzo dashed toward the front of the hotel and jumped into the Jeep.

"How are we going to go north-east?" Andrea asked. "There may not be a path in that direction."

"Then we'll make one…somehow," Brandon answered as he backed up and put the Jeep in forward, heading north-east. "Oh shit!" Brandon said to Lorenzo. "Please jump out and go get a walkie talkie from our room."

Lorenzo quickly hopped from the jeep and bounded up the front steps of the hotel.

Brandon laughed a small, nervous laugh. "In all the excitement, I almost forgot," he said.

"It's okay, Brandon," Andrea said, reaching over to rub his arm. "Just calm down a little."

"Calm down?" Brandon repeated. "Naja is alive. Dear God, how I was worried that she might be…"

"I know, I know."

Lorenzo returned at a trot with the walkie talkie, jumped in the back seat of the jeep and they were on their way.

There was a trail, as such, which headed more or less northward to an Indian village. The searchers had no choice except to follow that trail and hope it would bring them close enough to Naja that she could hear them yelling for her. Bruce launched Snoopy back in the air and floated over them, giving location updates on the walkie talkie.

Andrea chuckled as she looked up at the drone.

"What's so funny?" Brandon asked.

"I was just thinking," she said. "Here, in this *most* primitive, *most* ancient jungle, a space age electronic implement is being used to solve a problem. Just the meshing between the two. I… well, never mind. It's just that I remember when I first started coming to Central America, trying to make a phone call might take as long as three days, and then it sounded like you were on the moon."

"Yeah, I remember that too," Brandon said. "It's an interesting point well taken."

A few minutes later, Bruce's voice came over the walkie talkie, "Brandon, she's about a thousand yards to your left. Is there any way you can go that direction?"

"I don't know," Brandon answered.

"I'm seeing something that looks like a trail just ahead of you. You might not be able to drive the Jeep through there, but I think the trail is clear enough that you can walk. If you take it, I will guide you."

"Fantastic idea," Brandon said. They moved the Jeep slowly forward until they found the trail. Then they hopped out and began walking down the narrow path through the jungle. Brandon carried the walkie talkie. Bruce's voice suddenly announced, "Your team is headed directly toward her, Brandon. Just keep going in the direction you're headed. *Do not vary!*"

Brandon looked up to see Snoopy hovering high above. At this point, he started yelling Naja's name. It wasn't long before he heard the low, coughing roar of a jaguar, *his* jaguar. Brandon was beside himself with relief. He yelled her name again. Again, she roared. This time she sounded closer, and he could hear the sound of an animal running toward them, through the underbrush.

Then, almost like a vision, there she was, about fifty feet away. When she saw Brandon, she dashed forward and launched herself in a giant leap, landing on her master. The impact sent them both crashing into the brush, onto the jungle floor. Brandon didn't care, He had his Naja back. That was all that mattered. He hugged his cat and kissed her head as he spoke to her. The two of them rolled around on the ground like kids.

After rubbing herself all over Brandon, Naja then made her way to Andrea and then Lorenzo, telling them in her jaguar way that she loved them too.

But Naja had a surprise. She had a friend. And her friend had followed her, at least this far. He stood in a small clearing some fifty feet away and watched, obviously confused by Naja's strange behavior with these humans. He was a very handsome, heavy bodied male jaguar. He was not black like Naja, but rather, a beautiful, rich colored, rosetted animal.

Spotting him, Brandon said to Naja, "Girl, is this your friend?"

And then Brandon did what only Brandon, in the whole world can do. He called to the wild jungle cat and motioned. At first, the large male jaguar hesitated. Then he carefully paced forward until he was at Brandon's feet. Brandon stared at the animal, and it seemed to understand. It looked up at him as he scratched it behind the ears and spoke to it in some very strange sounding language.

Andrea and Lorenzo, stood by, motionless, watching the scene before them, smiling, in awe. Although, neither of them was surprised. They knew of the special abilities Brandon possessed with animals.

Brandon could now hear the drone above him. Bruce was apparently dropping Snoopy down for a closer look. After a minute or so, Brandon expected the wild jaguar to turn and escape back into the jungle. But that is not what was happening. The male jaguar started to follow when the party began their trek back toward the Jeep.

At first, Brandon didn't notice. But Andrea, walking behind him said, "Brandon! Look behind you!" Brandon stopped and turned. There, right behind Naja, was the male jaguar, following along as if he were a puppy.

"I'll be damned!" Brandon said, as a smile widened on his face. Then he looked at the male jaguar and said, "What's going on here? Are you wanting to go with us?"

He bent down to cuddle both jaguars, Naja in his left arm, the big male in his right.

Andrea said, under her breath, "Why in the world didn't I bring my camera? I would give my left foot for a picture of this."

"This jaguar has been around people," Brandon said.

"How do you know?" Andrea asked.

"Well, sometimes when Indians kill a jaguar for its pelt, they discover that the jaguar is a female and has cubs, or a cub. Indian's are tied to the jungle and believe that to leave the cub to die would be a mortal sin which would come back to haunt them. So, they take the cub home and care for it until it gets too big to feed. When that happens, they take it back into the jungle and teach it how to hunt, then abandon it, just as it's mother would have done. But the jaguar remembers. Then, if it ever encounters humans again, something like this happens."

"Amazing!" Andrea said. "So, what are we going to do?"

Brandon continued to scratch the male jaguar on the head. After several moments he stood up, looked at Andrea and said, "Take him home."

Andrea knew it would do no good to argue. She just nodded her head and said, smiling, "I just knew that's what you were going to say. Jesus help us! Okay, let's go."

CHAPTER FIVE

Naja Comes Home...With A Friend

WHEN THEY RETURNED TO THE JUNGLE INN, BRUCE BURNS WAS pacing back and forth on the hotel landing waiting for them. As soon as Brandon got out of the Jeep and started walking up the steps, Bruce flanked him saying excitedly, yet smiling while he talked, "What the hell is this? I thought you only had one jaguar."

"Now I have two," Brandon said, offhandedly.

"Two?" Bruce said, looking around at the big cats. "Two! What do you mean? This other full grown, flipping jaguar just 'followed you home'?"

"Yeah, something like that."

"Great Caesar's Ghost!" Bruce said excitedly. I've never seen anything like this in my whole life. Who are you? What are you?"

"He's Brandon Shaw," Andrea said, mimicking Kan-Bah's stoic line.

"Ah, there's really no big mystery," Brandon said with a coy smile. Then he repeated his explanation, this time for Bruce. "Many times, although it's against the law, the Indians kill a jaguar for its pelt. Sometimes that jaguar is a female who has a cub. When that happens, the Indian's family feels obligated to raise the cub until it gets big enough to take care of itself. Otherwise, their soul is condemned to eternal hell. It's the *real* law of the jungle.

"Eventually, the cub gets too big for them to take care of, so, they return it to the jungle. But the jaguar never forgets. If it encounters a human and the human doesn't panic…well, you see the result."

"I sure do see it! I thought I would shit my pants when you bailed out of that Jeep with *two* jaguars following you. Oops. Excuse my language, Ma'am," he said, looking over at Andrea.

"No problem," Andrea said, smiling to herself because she knew the real truth.

Bruce looked down at Naja. "An absolutely beautiful cat. Stunning. Acts more like a tabby than a jaguar." Then, "Hello, girl. Welcome back! Your daddy sure is glad to have you home. The rest of us are too."

Bruce stayed with the group as they entered the restaurant and took seats at a table where Kan-Bah was already seated.

Didier was there to greet Naja with a good head rub. He looked at Naja and said, "We were all very worried about you, girl. And who is your new friend?"

Observing all this, Bruce said, "You know, every one of you talk to this jaguar like she is a golden retriever instead of a jaguar, one that understands you. That isn't all that unusual, but what is seems to be the fact that she *does* understand. What's all that about?"

"Naja was raised by me from a tiny cub," Brandon explained honestly. "She senses the intonations of voices, whether somebody is being friendly, stern or what have you. So, her reactions are a response to that."

Andrea interrupted. "Don't look now, boys and girls, but we have two extremely huge mouths to feed instead of one. And I believe the second addition to our group needs a name."

Lorenzo said, "Let's name him, 'Brand'."

Andrea looked at Lorenzo. "Brand?" What kind of a name is that?"

"Bueno. B R from Brandon, A N D from Andrea. Brand!"

Andrea rolled her eyes. "Lorenzo, I love you, my dear, dear friend, but that's a silly name. We're not going to have a three-hundred, plus pound, male jaguar running around the hotel named 'Brand'."

Lorenzo got a little defensive. "Okay. That was my suggestion. What's yours?"

"Cisco!" Didier said from the sidelines.

Brandon nodded. "That has a ring to it. All in favor of Cisco?"

Everybody raised their hand, including Lorenzo.

Brandon looked at the big male jaguar and said, "My friend, you now have a name. You will be known as, Cisco. So be it. It is done."

Brandon paused, then said to Bruce, "Let's switch the subject for a minute, not to diminish my gratitude for your invaluable help in finding my cat. How did you get here from The Lost City? Did you fly in? I didn't hear any helicopter."

"No," Bruce stated. "I drove here along the new road, if you want to call it that."

"New road?"

"Yeah. The Honduran government approved a road to be bulldozed through the jungle so that researchers could more easily access The Lost City with heavy equipment that is too big and heavy to put on a chopper."

"Really! That's hard to believe. So, how far is it from here, in hours, to The Lost City, by vehicle of course?"

"On a lucky day, four. But the 'road' is so narrow you had better hope you don't meet someone coming from the other direction, like a truck, Jeep, or even a large turtle! If you do, chances are you both will have to get out and chop a place in the brush wide enough that you can go around each other."

"Is there that much traffic on the road?"

"No. That's the good news, and the bad news. If your vehicle runs out of gas or worse, halfway between here and there, you're a sunk duck."

"We'll keep that in mind."

"Why? Is, The Lost City where you're bound?"

"I'm afraid so," Brandon confessed.

Bruce leaned back in his rattan chair. "Really. Are you researchers? Archaeologists?"

"No," Brandon confessed. "We're on a different kind of mission."

Bruce sat in silence, waiting for the other shoe to drop. He was too polite to be intrusively nosy, but his curiosity was driving him crazy. Why would anyone go to the trouble to gain access to this almost impossible spot on earth other than research? Surely it couldn't be tourist curiosity. Even to get this far along that jungle road was a trial by torture.

Brandon took a deep sip of his drink. Then, "If I told you, you would need every bottle behind that bar over there to wrap your head around it. Anyway, thank you for helping save my Naja. I really do owe you."

"No, you don't," Bruce said. "The pleasure was mine. And like I said, just seeing this beautiful animal back home safely is enough reward for me. It touches my heart. And the new Cisco is a bonus. I can't get over it. Looking at him lying there next to Naja, you'd think he had been part of this, 'family,' forever. I do hope you don't mind if I take a couple of pictures. I mean, my wife…"

"No problem. So, how long were you at The Lost City?" Brandon asked.

"I was there about a week," Bruce answered. "That was long enough."

"What do you mean by that?"

"I mean there are some pretty strange things going on there. Things that will run a chill up the bravest man's spine."

Bruce had started petting Naja, and therefore had his focus on her. But Brandon waited for the rest of the truth to come out.

Finally, Bruce said, "Brandon (long pause), Jesus! I can't believe I'm saying this out loud. Let me ask you a question. Do you believe in ghosts?"

"Why do you ask?" Brandon said.

Bruce stood up and turned slightly away. "Because... because. Oh, never mind. It's just too fantastic to believe. I don't believe it myself and I was there. I saw it."

"Come on now," Brandon chided. "You can't start a story like that and not finish it. It's bad manners. It's like starting a good joke and then forgetting the punch line."

"Oh! This is no joke," Bruce said. "You're going to think I'm as crazy as a shit house rat."

"Well, at least you're among friends. I think we're all a little bit bananas around here."

Bruce thought about it for a minute, then sat back down in his chair. "Okay, here goes. I'm not crazy. At least, I don't think I am. There are... 'ghosts' at that archaeological site. Ghosts, spirits, poltergeists, hell, I don't know what to call them. The whole place is up to the rafters with them. I've been to a lot of Maya sites. I mean, a lot of Maya sites. I've seen a lot, but I've never encountered anything like I did at The Lost City of The Monkey God. I've never been so glad to get away from a place in my life. Before I went there, they gave me inoculations, and told me to be careful about not getting some kind of flesh-eating fungus that would eat my face off. I thought they were pulling my leg about that. As it turned out, they weren't. But nobody and I mean nobody said anything about ghosts."

Bruce then looked at everyone around the table. "You all

think I've lost it, don't you? You think I've gone 'around the bend'. I, I don't blame you. I know how it must sound."

Everyone assured Bruce they did not, almost simultaneously.

"Just relax, my friend," Brandon said, placing his hand on Bruce's shoulder. "Nobody thinks you've lost your mind. So, kick back, let's have a couple of Didier's special Jungle Juices, sing Jingle Bells and get sloppy. We've all earned it, you and Snoopy most of all."

"Thank you," Bruce said gratefully. Leaning back in the rattan chair and getting comfortable. Bruce then added, as a casual thought, "You know, there was another guy there who left The Lost City a few days before me. Sam… something. He saw the same thing I did, but it really put a weed up his…back side, spooked him bad, made him freak. The last anybody saw of him, he was blowing out of there in a cloud of dust, driving a Jeep similar to the one parked out front. At first, I thought it was his. But I haven't seen him around here. Such a damn shame. He was one of the nicest people you would ever hope to meet. But seeing those 'things' whatever they are, really spooked him. Forgive the term."

"He was here," Brandon admitted.

"He was? Where is he now?"

"He got drunker than Cooter Brown and started shooting a canon sized pistol at Naja. Wrong thing to do. I 'intervened' and sent him packing."

"Why do I feel like this story is going to have a bad ending?"

"Was he a close friend of yours?"

"No. I just met him at The Lost City. He seemed very nice, at first. But when he saw those green things, like I say, it spooked him and he started drinking, didn't sleep. It was like watching two sides of somebody, or maybe somebody possessed. He just seemed to lose touch with reality. To tell you the truth, as drunk as he was, I'm surprised to see that he managed to drive successfully along that jungle road, with all its twists and turns."

Bruce saw everybody looking at one another. "So," he asked, "Where is he now?"

"Don't know," Brandon admitted. I kicked his ass pretty badly, then dragged him out in the front parking lot. I was furious about him shooting at Naja. At that point, I didn't know if he had killed her, or what. I gave him a choice of taking off down the road, or I would use that damned revolver of his on him. He chose wisely and hit the road. It was night, very dark. No telling what he got into."

"Good Lord," Bruce blurted. "Alone? Injured? In the jungle, and this is not a nice jungle. There's lots of very deadly snakes out there, to say nothing of the other creatures."

"True," Brandon said, knowingly.

Bruce thought in silence for several minutes, sitting, sipping his drink, staring at the Christmas tree. "You know, I'm not saying that you weren't right to protect what is yours, and I can certainly understand about Naja. But, I've got to tell you, I feel sorry for Sam. I saw the real Sam before he got the hell scared out of him by those things at The Lost City. The Sam I saw was a good person."

"So, what is it you want to do?"

"Well, honestly, I think I've got to try to find him."

"Yeah. That's what I thought you were going to say." Brandon said. "So, what are you going to do *if* you find him, and *if* he's still alive?"

"Well, I should try to get him back here, I suppose. Give him some first aid, make him comfortable, then, depending on the severity of his injuries, maybe try to get a Life Flight helicopter to come in here and extract him, take him to a hospital."

"So now I guess it's our turn to try and help you."

"I guess so, but I don't know how. I'm going to get Snoopy in the air, if you'll tell me what direction he was going when you last saw him."

Brandon sighed with resignation. "Naw. Forget that, at least for now. I think I know a better way. But first, I want to give you my opinion about something. I am going to help you. Not only because I owe you, but because you are a nice guy. But your friend Sam is not a nice guy. Any person who would hurt an animal is an evil degenerate. I don't care what the circumstances might be. For instance, alcohol is no excuse. 'Sam' is a cad in my book. Now, I won't say anything else about it. But as you go through life, beware of people who don't like animals, or people that animals don't like. Animals have a special sense about good people versus bad."

Then Brandon did something that only Brandon Shaw, in the whole wide world can do. He got face to face with Naja and spoke to her in their secret language. After a minute, Naja turned and darted out the front of the hotel, followed closely by Cisco. They quickly turned right and disappeared out of sight.

Bruce looked at Brandon, very puzzled by what he had just seen. "What the hell was that? What did you just do?"

"I told her to go search for Sam," Brandon said. "Then come back here and lead us to him. He couldn't be very far away. He's hurt too badly. I just hope he's still alive. Well, sorta hope, anyway."

"No, no. What I mean is…what? Wait a minute. You're telling me that you just communicated all that information to Naja? You *talked* to that jaguar? And the jaguar understood!"

"Yeah. So?"

"That's all you've got to say? 'Yeah, so'? I don't mean any disrespect, God knows, but just who the hell are you, anyway?"

"Brandon Shaw," he said, winking at Andrea

Bruce looked around the room at everyone present, all of

whom had a knowing smile on their face, and who were chuckling at Bruce's 'awakening'.

"When I get home and tell my wife about some of the things I've seen on this trip, she's gonna have me committed," Bruce said, and sank back in his chair and took a deep sip of his drink.

"Pedro," Bruce said despairingly, "May I have another Jungle Juice, please? And make it strong!" Then, talking to himself, he said, "He just had a 'chat' with a jaguar. No big deal. Hey! They play poker together."

Naja returned in a short time and sat at Brandon's feet. Cisco joined her. Brandon looked at Naja intently as she made mewing sounds. Bruce watched in fascinated awe.

At last, Brandon sat back in his chair. "She found him. Apparently, he isn't too far from here. He's alive but Naja says 'the man sleeps'. Not sure what that means. We'd better go fetch him. Bruce, Lorenzo, you come with me. Andrea, you and Didier can prepare a bed for him...and probably a bath. Kan-Bah, can you just stand by for whatever other help we need?"

"Of course," Kan-Bah said. "Kan-Bah will do whatever is required to assist."

With that, the trio, accompanied by Naja and Cisco, walked to the front of the hotel and got in the Jungle Cargo Jeep. Naja sat in the front passenger seat beside Brandon, because he had to follow her prompts in order to find the missing man.

This was accomplished by Brandon traveling in whatever direction Naja looked. Then, at one point, Naja started fidgeting and looking off to the left of the Jeep. Brandon stopped and Naja, accompanied by Cisco, jumped out, going around the Jeep and dashing off the road, where the Jeep could not travel.

They found Sam about fifty yards away, at the base of a

tree. He was not in good shape. He was unconscious with ants crawling all over him. They managed to brush the insects off of him as well as possible, then carry him to the Jeep.

Back at the hotel, everyone pitched in to get the injured man clean, then offered first aid as best as they could. But it was obvious that the archaeologist was badly injured and needed professional medical attention.

Bruce made an emergency call on his special satellite phone, and within two hours, a life flight helicopter arrived, then quickly took off from the Jungle Inn with Sam and Bruce on board. Sam was in rough shape, but according to the medics on board the chopper, he would make it. Everybody including Pedro the bartender stood on the landing of the hotel and watched the helicopter lift off.

"And thus endeth another chapter in the life of Brandon Shaw," Andrea said as the chopper disappeared over the treetops.

"Is that your way of saying, all's well that ends well?" Brandon asked.

"At least it did this time," Andrea said. "It could have been worse."

"Yeah," Brandon admitted. "A lot worse. At least the asshole is still alive. Wonder if he learned a lesson?" The group turned and walked back to the restaurant/bar.

"I learned something about myself, from this little incident," Brandon said.

"Yeah? What's that?" Andrea asked.

"I learned just how deeply I can feel things."

"I thought you already knew that."

"Not completely. I've learned all sorts of things about myself since falling in love with you." Brandon smiled at Andrea.

"I think it is now time for a Christmas celebration," Andrea said, smiling back at Brandon, as she slipped her arm around his waist. She got a quick, rousing round of approval.

"Egg-nog, everybody, egg-nog! Didier said enthusiastically.

"Egg-nog?" Andrea said, surprised. "Didier, we're in the middle of the jungle. Where…oh never mind."

Didier smiled a broad smile. "I am a long way from being out of magic," he said, and laughed.

CHAPTER SIX

Road to The Lost City

THE NEWLY BULLDOZED ROAD LEADING THROUGH THE JUNGLE from The Jungle Inn to The Lost City of The Monkey God was indeed narrow. Broken branches of plants and trees, cleared by the bulldozer which graded the road, frequently scraped the sides of the Jeep and the old blue truck as they made their way along. At least, the absence of any vehicular traffic on the road left it in good shape as far as pot-holes were concerned. So, the ride wasn't too jarring, just twisting, back and forth. This was actually a down-stream result of the Honduran government's dictates when granting the permit to construct a road in this national forest. They stipulated that no large trees be felled. It was their attempt at conservation, preservation of the national forest, and a good one insofar as the jungle was concerned. Just not so hot from the standpoint of clearing a road.

The downstream effect was that the bulldozers had to work their way around the big trees, mostly kapok, sapodilla and mahogany. This doubled the distance, at a minimum. But in the jungle, one learns to deal with things, not bitch about them. Not that bitching would do any good. So why bother?

Although the distance was far, no one seemed to mind too badly because driving along this road was like watching a very exotic video in 3D. The road shared one thing in common with the other road which led into the jungle from the West side of the Mosquitia. The jungle canopy closed in overhead and shaded the way, although here, it was not nearly as low and confining as on the western side of the Jungle Inn.

Beneath this canopy, every form of animal in Central America roamed, unafraid of man because they had never seen man, had no experience with him, ergo no fear. Watching them as they stared back was an interesting lesson in nature.

Spider monkeys hung from vines, by their tails, very close to the bulldozed road and watched with curiosity as the two-vehicle convoy passed. Even the birds here hesitated to take flight, vying instead to stay their perch for a closer look at these strange creatures who had come to visit in their forest home.

Didier had asked to come along on this journey, perhaps because of curiosity, perhaps because in his own way, he felt like he was the de facto governor here in this labyrinth and wanted to keep his finger on the pulse of his jungle domain.

In any case, he sat in the back seat, sharing it with Naja, contentedly looking around as they slowly made their way along, even waving to some of the animals and whistling at them or saying hello as they passed.

For this leg of the trip, the only place for Cisco to ride was in the back of the truck with the sarcophagus. One might compare it to 'economy class,' but it was the only space they had to offer, for now.

Occasionally they would see a large boa constrictor or even a fer-de-lance crossing the narrow road. Brandon would pause his vehicle, allowing the creature to get safely out of the way instead of running over it. On one occasion, a family of coati mundis was walking along the road; a papa, mamma and three youngsters, their ringed tails uniformly erect, being held straight up like flagpoles as they padded along.

Brandon slowed his Jeep to a crawl, not wanting to disturb them. After all, this was their home, not his. He was only a visitor. Eventually, the coatis found a place where they wanted to turn left, off of the road, and disappeared into the underbrush.

"I wonder if the Garden of Eden was anything like this," Brandon said, softly.

"I don't know," Andrea answered. "But it sure feels like being at the beginning of the world. Look at the thousands of orchids and bromeliads. Look at those huge iridescent blue butterflies," she said, excitedly pointing. "Smell that air. It's so fresh. So...rich with oxygen!" Andrea spread her arms open wide, tilted her head back and inhaled deeply.

And so, the convoy progressed through the Mosquitia Jungle, in no rush as they absorbed this journey through a timeless world. The beauty and the emotions inspired by it were kaleidoscopic, accompanied by a lot of pointing and editorial comments.

Four hours later, the road abruptly widened, then ended and emptied into an expansive cleared area where most of the smaller trees had been cut down, leaving only the big ones. They had arrived. The travelers found themselves at The Lost City of The Monkey God.

It was a cluttered archaeological site with numerous stone structures, buildings, pyramids, temples, some buildings that looked as though they may have been used for government purposes, all scattered throughout the jungle, helter-skelter; or at least, seemingly so to the untrained eye. The topography was low, rolling hills, all covered with dense jungle. And all of it dotted with relics of a lost city that was once vibrant, albeit well over a thousand years ago.

Andrea visually scanned the area. She had been here once

before, but she wasn't sure that counted. Everything seemed different somehow. Or maybe she was just seeing things from a different mind-set, a different perspective.

There was a strong smell of 'green' in the air, the fresh, sweet aroma of chlorophyll. It was late December, and the plants here were blooming, putting out pollen and adding new leaves. How strange, she thought. Back in Indiana, they would be up to their knees in snow. Here, they were fighting the heat.

Continuing her visual scan, she observed stone carved statues, stela, monuments and potsherds scattered on the ground everywhere, plus a collection of carved stone effigies of what the archaeologists had dubbed, the 'Were-Jaguar.' There was also a large contingent of scientists and researchers, judging from the number of tents and 'Easy-up' covers, used to shade tables covered with certain finds that the researchers wanted to keep from getting wet during rain.

Still, something did not look right. Researchers, both men and women seemed to be idle, milling around in the central area where their encampment was established, as though they were intentionally stalling, killing time. A tall man in his forties walked toward Brandon, then extended his hand in greeting as he approached.

"Hello there. I'm Brad Harding," the man said. Brandon introduced himself and made all other introductions as his group got down from the two vehicles and started to stretch their legs. Brad Harding was slightly taken aback when he saw two full grown jaguars join the group.

"Is it my imagination, or is something 'out of place' happening here?" Brandon asked.

Brad Harding looked over his shoulder at the assemblage of people aimlessly milling around. Then he looked back at Brandon. "I'm afraid we have a very odd situation on our hands," Brad said in a heavy British accent. "Let's see how I can put this. It's rather hard to talk about because it borders on the fantastic. Well, here goes! Basically, there are ancient souls here who manifest themselves. They actually appear with such regularity that we believe they have an agenda. I'm aware that sounds like I, or all of us have lost our minds, but there it is."

Brandon looked at Andrea and back to Brad. "Ghosts, with an agenda?"

"Yes, I know how it sounds. Crazy! Welcome to The Twilight Zone! A ghost is hard enough to accept. But when you add the possible element of an actual agenda. Well...it has caused quite a stir here, a lot of consternation. More than that, really. The whole camp is rather frozen with fear, frightened of excavating anywhere. Every time they do, one of those green things, whatever you want to call them, manages to crop up and raise cockles, or worse."

"What's a cockle?" Brandon asked

"Um, I think you call them goosebumps, raise the hair on the back of one's neck, that sort of thing. In other words, scare the living hell out of a person, or worse."

"Worse?"

"We've had a couple of strange heart attacks occur which required medical extraction via helicopter. And then we had one chap that just seemed to lose his wig entirely and went fleeing into the jungle in one of the organization's Jeeps."

"Was his name Sam?"

"Matter of fact, I think it was, yes. Sam Jeffreys, I think. Have you seen him?

"Yeah, long story. He's in the hospital. Your Jeep is safe at this man's hotel," Brandon indicated Didier, who waved hello."

"Extraordinary!" Brad said. "Poor fellow. In the hospital you say?"

"Yeah, he's safe, as far as I know. Look, we've got other things to concern ourselves with. This esteemed Maya looking gentleman who is with us is known as Kan-Bah, and he has a very important reason for being here. So, with your leave, for now, we're going to get on with what we have to do. No disrespect intended. But you know what, there may be a way that Kan-Bah can help you with your problem. Like I said, he is an 'extraordinary gentleman', to use your term."

"You don't say?" Brad said with sudden increased interest and taking a second, closer look at Kan-Bah.

With little ceremony, Kan-Bah walked to the back of the blue truck and untied the blue plastic tarp covering the sarcophagus, not that it was necessary. Lifting the plastic to one side, he placed his hand on the sarcophagus. He began speaking in an ancient Mayan language called 'Pech" that predated Quiche'. Then after speaking for a minute or so, he stopped and waited.

The apparition now identified as Spirit Sky, began to manifest and take shape outside of the sarcophagus. Moments later, there, beside the stone coffin that he had rode in, floating in air was the green duende. But it did not linger for long. In the next moment it streaked toward the structure where it was first discovered and was out of sight. It all happened so fast that people who didn't know what they were seeing weren't sure they had seen anything at all.

Kan-Bah walked over to Brandon, looked up at him and said, "The grateful duende is returned to his proper place. But we still have work to do."

Brandon looked at Kan-Bah, mildly astonished. "Work to do? What possible work could we have to do?"

"It is time for you to face the truth about yourself, Brandon Shaw. You are the reincarnation of Ba'alam Ma'ax. Ba'alam Ma'ax was the great ruler of this city almost two thousand years ago. You are Ba'alam Ma'ax; reborn in a different time, and in a different shape, but still of the same soul."

"How do you know that?" Brandon demanded. "How the hell does anybody know that? Is reincarnation even real? In case you haven't noticed by now, I'm a Christian. We're taught that when you croak, your soul goes to heaven, and I believe that."

Kan-Bah smiled. "Please forgive me. Once again, I must quote the famous bard; 'There are more things in heaven and on earth, Horatio, than are dreamt of in your philosophy.' Hamlet (1.5.167-8). And for the record, I am a Christian also."

Brandon stared down at the short man in mild shock. "Who are you? One minute you sound and look like an old Quiche' wise man. The next minute, you sound like an Oxford professor."

"I am Kan-Bah," Kan-Bah said.

Didier smiled broadly, as if he were privy to an inside joke. Brandon looked away from Kan-Bah to Didier, then to Andrea and Lorenzo. It seemed as though everybody was waiting on something.

"What?" Brandon said to them all simultaneously. "I feel like the monkey in a one monkey side show here!"

"Hardly that," Kan-Bah said. "Let's all go exploring. This city is much too large to see it all, and the archaeologists have only begun to unveil its magnificent secrets. But I want to take you on a slow walk to see some of the things they have uncovered."

Kan-Bah headed into the archaeological site, walking stick in hand. The rest of the troupe followed like boy scouts behind a leader.

In the next few hours, Kan-Bah led his students through a labyrinth of stone structures, statues and of course, the basketball sized effigies of the 'were-jaguar' which were everywhere.

"Every one of these rocks on the ground had meaning to some poor Maya. To us, they are just rocks, to avoid and not be tripped over. To the Maya who quarried them, they represented a labor of devotion and most likely, love. The stone had to be carved, shaped in a specific size and then wedged into place with mortar as a part of something…most likely some structure. And I will remind you, the Maya had no metal tools. Every stone they quarried and shaped was accomplished with stone tools, most likely obsidian."

"Okay," Brandon said. I know about the obsidian. But where did they get obsidian? Obsidian is essentially a volcanic glass, right?"

"Yes."

"Well, there are no volcanos around here, or for hundreds of miles for that matter."

"From out there, on the water," Kan-Bah said, pointing in the direction of the Caribbean. "The Maya were great traders. They had trade routes set up all along this coast. They plied the waters in very large canoes, sometimes twenty meters long. Obsidian was in great demand, so it would have demanded a high price. I would imagine when they came here, they traded for jade, or jaguar pelts."

"Were they conscripted labor?" Andrea wanted to know.

"Most likely some of them were," Kan-Bah said. That was the general use for warriors captured during an inter-city battle for more land. But there were also artisans who were paid and took a great deal of pride in building this city. Actually, they were engineers who were quite educated and very skilled."

"Where did they obtain all this education?" Brandon asked.

"Good question," Kan-Bah answered. "Nobody knows for sure. Maybe they were self-taught. The Maya displayed an amazing grasp for numbers in many ways, and they were inventive to say the least."

"Then why didn't they ever invent the wheel?" Andrea asked. "The most basic of tools."

"Actually, they did invent the wheel," Kan-Bah countered. "They just never managed to put it to a practical use. They employed it abundantly in children's toys. But, first of all, the Maya had no beasts of burden; no donkeys, no horses. And secondly, they had no petroleum, no lubrication as such. In order to put the wheel to a practical use, it would have required that something be used to grease the axels."

"So…" Didier chimed in. "No grease, no rolling commerce. I guess antiquity accounts for the reason that, to this day, you see Maya Indians going down the road with huge loads on their backs, and the women balance heavy jars of water or coconut oil on their heads."

"So it would seem," Kan-Bah said.

Kan-Bah led his group up the side of a medium sized pyramid. The one he had chosen had a flat platform at its apex. He asked Brandon to accompany him up the steps to the top of the pyramid. Then he guided Brandon to the middle of the platform, instructed him to close his eyes and clear his mind.

"Now, with your eyes closed and your mind open, what do you see? I want you to smell and hear, Brandon Shaw." Kan-Bah asked, looking up at Brandon.

Brandon was silent for a few minutes. Then he said, "I don't see anything. But I hear the sounds of distant voices and I smell food cooking."

"Good!" Kan-Bah said. "You're getting there." He smiled at everybody in the group at the base of the small pyramid. "I think it is time. We must go to the place where you first encountered the duende."

"What for?" Brandon demanded, a little alarmed. "I thought we were done with that sonofabitch."

"Hardly," Kan-Bah said. "These restless souls who have been disturbed need your guidance. You must speak to them. You must channel through Spirit Sky."

"Speak to them? Speak to them about what? And how? What do you mean 'channel'? I wouldn't know how."

"Speak to them in Pech."

"Speak to them in Pech? What the hell is Pech? Is that a language? I don't speak Pech."

"You have spoken Pech for a long time, Brandon Shaw. What language do you think it is that you use when you communicate with the black jaguar, Naja?"

"Pech? That's Pech?"

"Come with me, Brandon Shaw." Then, turning to the others in the group, Kan-Bah said, "You may come too, if you wish. Witnesses would be helpful."

Andrea quickly took a place beside Brandon when he reached the base of the pyramid. "Are you kidding?" she said. "I wouldn't miss this for the world!"

The small group, led by Kan-Bah managed to wend their way through the stone debris and many structures of The Lost City of The Monkey God, to the site of the temple where Brandon and others first saw the original Duende, an apparent sub-ruler, a 'cacique' of The Lost City of The Monkey God, now identified as Spirit Sky.

The same battery-operated light system was still set up as had been there the last time Brandon and Andrea visited this place, several months ago. Kan-Bah did not know how to turn the lights on, so Brandon flipped the switch. Then the group entered and Kan-Bah led them to the same inner chamber where the sarcophagus rested containing the strange skeleton. The members of the party gathered around the stone coffin and peered inside.

The skeleton was of a person well over six feet tall and otherwise mostly normal except that the bones of the hands were in fact the bones of claws, jaguar claws. This was the skeleton of Ba'alam Ma'ax, Jaguar Man. The living being would have been a giant among the ancient Maya who were barely over four feet tall.

Kan-Bah looked across at Brandon. "You have been here before?"

Brandon silently nodded, yes.

"Your friend sought you out and brought you here to show you this. When you saw it, you rejected the evidence before you that bore the truth."

Brandon looked at Kan-Bah. "Truth? And how did you know it was me that was 'here before'? I'll tell you something else. I've got another question. This ass-hole, whoever he was, apparently had hands that were like jaguar claws. All of the stone effigies we've seen lying around here were of somebody with the head of jaguar. So how do you explain that?"

For the first time since he had met Kan-Bah, the man reeled and got a puzzled look on his face. "I don't know," he admitted.

"Well, I'll be damned!" Brandon said ironically. "The great Kan-Bah finally comes up against a question he doesn't have the answer to. This is a red-letter day."

"Why is that important?" Andrea asked.

"How could it not be? This guy is wanting to lead me down a garden path claiming I am the reborn incarnation of some freak with hands like a jaguar, but the apparent real big wig of this hoe-down was a dude with a *head* like a jaguar. A *head*! Not hands. And *that* fucker is the one that apparently had everybody's attention, because when I stop and think about it, I haven't seen one damn statue anywhere around here that is dedicated to 'hand job' here. So, what's up, Kan-Bah? The chips are down, brother. Inquiring minds want to know."

Kan-Bah turned away from the sarcophagus. He looked devastated. He braced himself against the inside wall of the structure for several moments, then uttered, "You are right. There is another alter-being, and we must track him down. I suspect that as with so many such instances, one was good, and one was evil. But which was which? We must make sure before we beseech either one of them. To bring forth the wrong one could be.... Well, it could be catastrophic."

"Well, that's just great," Brandon said, now indignant. "It's a good thing we caught this little glitch before we unleashed all hell on this place!"

Kan-Bah turned and looked at the furious Brandon. "I am sorry. But, you are most absolutely right. We did catch the mistake in time, Thank God, and thanks to you."

"Okay," Brandon said, a little calmer. "So now what do we do about it?"

"The first thing I'm going to do is go outside and get some fresh air," Kan-Bah said. "I need to consider what we have found out here. And I need to recover from what I fear I almost did. My God! I.."

The consensus of opinion was wholesale, and everybody walked out of the small pyramid into the fresh air.

"So, let me see if I've got this straight," Lorenzo mused. "Now you're saying there are two pinche' tigre mestizos. One might be good, and the other is a cabron?"

"Something like that," Didier said. "But in this case, the cabron one could end the world as we know it."

Lorenzo stared at Didier while making a strange expression. "And the problem is that we don't know which is which? Hijole! Is there any more shit we can stack on this tortilla?"

No one answered Lorenzo's throw-away question. But everyone did look to Kan-Bah for answers. Kan-Bah looked at the ground, then, up, into the air as if seeking wisdom. After a time, he said, "We must find the tomb of the other being."

Everyone heard Kan-Bah. And everyone looked at one another, but nobody said a word. Finally, it was Didier who broke the pregnant silence.

"Why? Are we looking for evidence of evil? That's it, isn't it? We are, aren't we?"

"Yes," Kan-Bah admitted. "And if we find evil, we must make sure we do not release it."

"Then why look for it?" Brandon demanded. "Seems like we're playing with fire here for no good reason."

"No. There is good reason. It is so that we can make sure whose spirit we are beseeching," Kan-Bah said defensively.

"Beseeching? What do you mean, 'beseeching'?" Brandon demanded. "I didn't know we were going to 'beseech' a goddamn thing. I'll tell you what, this whole thing is beginning to stink like a whorehouse at low tide."

"You're going to need help to transition, in order to communicate with Spirit Sky."

"Spirit Sky," Brandon said, almost with resignation. "Spirit Sky? You're talking about the guy we just gave a ride to halfway across Honduras in a stone taxi? That Spirit Sky?"

Brandon fell silent for several moments as if a thought was occurring to him. "Hey!" he said. "I've got it! Yes, there is 'another' creature here and that creature is a bad ass. But luckily, that skeleton right in there, in that room, is not of the bad one, that's the good one!"

"How do you know?" Andrea asked, stepping forward.

"That's what these ghosts have been afraid of all along. Have you ever heard of 'ghosts' jumping up and raising hell at any other Mayan archaeological site? And there are hundreds of other Mayan archaeological sites, lost cities, whatever you want to call them. No! There's never been so much as a hint of trouble. And you know why? Because not one of them had what this one has, a really bad, as in evil, mother that scares the shit out of them, even after a couple of thousand years."

"I think you are right," Kan-Bah said, "But we must be absolutely certain."

"Oh, I agree, one hundred percent," Brandon said. "But how do we make sure for certain?" After several minutes of thought, Brandon said in a voice barely audible at first, "The Maya had the only known written language in the new world at that time, and it was a pretty detailed language. We need to be investigators, just like these archaeologists around here. There is no way that either of these guys could have existed without the local scribe making a record of it."

"But Friar De Landa," Didier said.

"Aw, fuck Friar De Landa. He was a stupid, up tight sonofabitch, but the only thing he burned was books. First of all, I would be willing to bet that Friar De Landa couldn't read one swinging image of hieroglyphics. Second of all, I repeat because this is an important point, the only thing he ever burned were books.

"What I'm talking about is finding some stela, or glyphs carved on walls. There's got to be a record here somewhere. You can bet your last dollar on that. What we've got to do is find those glyphs. Now look, even if you can't read hieroglyphics, look for images depicting any personage with hands like jaguar paws, or a jaguar's head. That's your big clue, and that one gets you a star on your Mother Goose chart. Now spread out and search for all you are worth."

Thus, the search began. It would have been easier if the jungle growth had not been so close, so oppressive. Every member of the search party found themselves having to push leaf laden branches out of the way at every turn.

The extremely high humidity and heat didn't polish the apple any either. Everyone found themselves stopping every few minutes to sit on a flat stone and wring sweat from their shirt.

It was Lorenzo, about two hours into the hunt who started yelling repeatedly, "Aqui esta! It's here!"

"Where are you, Lorenzo?" Brandon yelled back at him.

"I don't know. Just follow my voice. Do you want me to sing?"

"Oh God, no!" Brandon said. "Anything but that. We're trying to keep that damn ghost in his tomb. If he hears you serenading, he'll be turning over in it."

He could hear Lorenzo laughing and used that as a beacon to find him, as did everyone else.

When the searchers found Lorenzo, they were stunned when they saw what he had found. He had pulled the jungle growth back that hid a huge boulder with a petroglyph clearly painted on it. There, facing each other were two large figures. The one on the left had large paws, like a jaguar. The one on the right had the head of a jaguar.

Hieroglyphics etched into the boulder beneath the two standing figures translated roughly to say that these were the ba'laam twins, and they represented good and evil. It also said that it was forbidden to make records of them, only effigies. No other record would be found.

There was a warning to beware of Kah, the Evil One with the head of a jaguar, that he consigned those who inspired his ire to the lower world. To disturb his resting place would release him and begin a 'black sun'.

When the deciphering was completed and everyone agreed on its meaning, Brandon plopped down on the ground, hard.

"I knew there was a hateful sonofabitch behind that, that damned jaguar head. 'Were Jaguar!' My guess is, he had the people around here terrified. The question is, why didn't they run? Why did they stay here?"

"Maybe they were afraid to run," Andrea said." Afraid of what that thing would do to them if they tried."

"So, their entire life was to be this thing's slave in one way or the other? If he needed labor to build another pyramid, they did it. If he wanted a virgin to sacrifice for that pyramid, they provided it. I wonder what it ate? And I wonder if it ever had offspring?

"So, where did this place get the name referring to a Monkey God?" Didier asked. "Looks to me like the dominating figure around here was a jaguar-person, or whatever."

"I've wondered about that too," Brandon said. "Imagine if

you will that somebody, a long time ago, somebody like a Spaniard, for instance, because it's said they are the first ones to spot this place and they called it the 'White City'. Imagine if you will, there was a large statue of this jaguar bastard, but the Spaniard thought it was a statue of an erect monkey, never thinking of something like a were-jaguar, because that would have been too fantastic for a Spaniard's limited way of thinking.

"Makes sense," Andrea said.

"Brandon," Kan-Bah said. "You are very astute. You were right all along."

"Yeah, I know, I'm right," Brandon said definitely. "The Jaguar Bastard, that's my name for him. He, 'it', is the reason these poor souls…excuse the pun, have been up in arms. They aren't worried about normal discoveries. They're afraid these bozos will inadvertently, and inevitably, come across the…let's call it, for now, '*The Forbidden Tomb*'. If that happens, and these well-intentioned yaks manage to peel the lid off of Bad Boy Bastard Jaguar, no telling what kind of evil they might unleash."

"Brandon, you've managed to save the day," Didier said with an amazed smile. "Well, no. This man has saved far more than just the day. There is no limit to what he may have saved. He has certainly saved all of our lives and the lives of everyone at The Lost City. And depending on who this evil spirit is, he may have saved all of mankind."

"Okay, working on the theory that I am right, and I think it's a pretty good bet that I am," Brandon said, "What do we do next?"

Without a word, Kan-Bah led everyone back into the small pyramid, to the open sarcophagus. Once everyone was gathered around the ancient skeleton, looking at Brandon, Kan-Bah said, "The first thing you must do here today is acknowledge that this was you almost two thousand years ago.

You were the ruler of this great city. You were Jaguar Man. You *must* accept it. Take the bones of the claws of the skeleton into your hands, hold them and close your eyes. When you do, you will see clearly into the past. The truth will be made known to you."

Brandon looked at Kan-Bah, then at Andrea, then peered at the skeleton intently. Would that explain why he had a special connection with animals? Would it explain how he just 'knew' a strange language that animals seemed to understand? A language that had never been taught to him by anybody?

Slowly, Brandon bent over and took the bones of the claws into his hands and held them.

"If you say so," he said to Kan-Bah. Then, "Just out of curiosity, do you know how I died?"

"Old age," Kan-Bah said. "Nothing could kill you. You lived over two hundred years."

"Hmmm. The Methuselah of Mayas!" Brandon said. He then closed his eyes as instructed. Suddenly Kan-Bah's voice faded and Brandon felt a jolt go through him as if he had grabbed hold of a hot electrical wire. He tried to scream in fear, but wasn't sure any sound had come from him. He was falling through a tunnel where he had absolutely no control. And then he arrived at a place where he had utter, total control.

He was Ba'alam Ma'ax, Jaguar Man. And he was the absolute unquestioned ruler over his domain. He stood at the entrance of a temple atop a steep pyramid looking down at the multitudes of subservient followers, all dressed in brightly colored clothing.

The followers looked up at him as if waiting for his holy words. And he, Jaguar Man, was adorned in jaguar pelts, crowned by an elaborate headdress made of quetzal feathers with bracelets of seashells tied around his legs just below the knees.

At last, he did raise his left arm, hand extended. But it was not a hand, it was a huge jaguar paw, complete with razor sharp amber colored claws, now extended for emphasis.

Brandon heard a voice thunder forth that he assumed was his own, speaking in an ancient dialect. But he understood it perfectly. "This day will be a day of feasting as we watch the sun cross the sky. But the Gods of this forest have demanded a sacrifice; the sacrifice of an enemy warrior And, so it must be."

At that moment, a young man, naked except for a leather loin cloth, his hands bound behind his back, emerged from the temple door, walked to where Jaguar Man stood and knelt on his knees before him, bowing his head.

Jaguar Man said, "Noble enemy, are you ready to give your life this day?"

The young man nodded his head affirmatively.

Jaguar Man motioned to a rectangular limestone block. The young man rose and walked to the stone, laid down on it and prepared to die. His heart would be cut from his living body and held up high by the royal priest. Who was also the official executioner. The heart would be shown to the crowd below, and they would cheer.

The priest appeared from within the temple, dressed in elaborate royal raiment's adorned with many quetzal feathers. He carried in his right hand, a large, black bladed obsidian dagger. He loomed over the young man, spoke briefly to the crowd below, and then, clutching the dagger in both hands, he raised his arms straight up and prepared to plunge the dagger into his victim. As the dagger made its swift trip downward, Brandon awoke from his vision, screaming.

Andrea rushed the few feet to him, grabbed him and held him in her arms in an effort to calm him. Brandon continued to scream at the top of his lungs for a few minutes longer, attempting to bring himself back to the present, back to reality.

He sagged to the ground, in a sitting position, gasping for air. Finally, he managed to start speaking in a quavering voice.

"Mother fucker! What was I, some kind of a blood thirsty, cut-throat, sonofabitch murderer?"

"Not at all. You were the ruler of this city," Kan-Bah said. "Tell me what you saw."

Brandon, hanging on to Andrea for support, began to detail what he had seen in his vision. When he reached the end, Kan-Bah began to explain.

"I thought you had studied the Maya," he started.

"Yeah, so?" Brandon replied.

"Then surely you know that the ancient Maya relied heavily on sacrifice to 'nourish their Gods'."

"Is that supposed to make me happier? If that was really me, I ordered the murder of a young man. He couldn't have been more than fifteen, maybe sixteen years old. My God!" He laid his head on Andrea's arm and began to weep.

"You cannot change what was, Brandon Shaw. But at this moment in time, you have a chance to put all of these lost spirits at rest and do some good. You and you alone can prevent more killing, by the spirits, and by 'the' spirit."

"Wait a minute," Brandon pleaded. I've got to get a handle on this. Who the hell were these people, half human, half jaguar? I mean, obviously they weren't normal, even for their period in time."

Kan-Bah thought for a minute. "There is an ancient legend from before the time of the Maya, from the Olmec in Tabasco, Mexico. They claimed their race was created when a spirit jaguar descended from the sky and mated with an Indian princess. Then just as suddenly as that legend appeared, it seemed to stop, go nowhere. It became sort of an Olmec version of a totem pole. That would have been about two thousand years ago."

"So, what are you suggesting?" Didier asked.

"I'm not sure," Kan-Bah said. "The apex of the Maya world was slightly west of here, in the Yucatan. And the Maya were the creators of the only known written language of that time, hieroglyphics. And those hieroglyphics were very good, very detailed. But when the Spaniards came to the Yucatan in the 1600 hundreds, there was a truly evil man named Friar Diego De Landa who, one fine July night stacked up every Maya text he could find and set it on fire. Thousands of years of irretrievable history was destroyed. Chances are the answers we seek were burned on that infamous night. Lost to us and lost to the world forever."

Andrea looked at Kan-Bah. "So, you're saying there was most likely a written account about the aberrations, the mixed human/jaguar beings?"

"I'm guessing. But yes."

"You're guessing? Then guess further."

"The Lost City of The Monkey God is the eastern-most Mayan civilization so far as we know or has ever been discovered. I think those 'aberrations' as you put it, were brought here. Tabasco is on the east coast of Mexico. The people who lived there were merchants who transported their goods by sea in the same very large, sea faring canoes that I told you about. It would not have been a stretch for them to have gone north, around the Yucatan peninsula, then east as far as they could go along that coast if they wanted to get rid of something they were afraid to kill. Or perhaps they couldn't kill it.

"Maybe they were afraid to kill them, or 'it'. Instead, they came as far east as they dared in canoes, abandoned 'it' in the jungle, thinking nature would take care of the problem. But that isn't what happened. 'It' survived. More than that, it thrived, flourished. This city came into being. That's what I'm guessing."

"Wow!" Lorenzo said with a whistle. "That's some pretty deep pinche' guessing."

"I'm not sure what all of that does to help the situation at hand," Kan-Bah said. "We've still got to deal with the immediate problem. And you, Don Brandon, have got to do it."

"How?" Brandon said, still gasping for air. "At this point I'm ready to do anything so long as it means we can get the fuck out of here."

Kan-Bah smiled for the very first time. "Follow me," he said.

Kan-Bah then led the group back into the small pyramid, but this time to the inner chamber of the pyramid where the green apparition first made its appearance.

Brandon looked around, slightly confused. "Okay, so what are we doing here?" he asked Kan-Bah.

"Our passenger spirit is about to reappear," Kan-Bah said calmly. "When he does, he will be looking to you for guidance. You are the only person who can do this. You now know, you are the rebirth of Ba'alam Ma'ax, but the duende only sees his ancient leader when he looks at you. He is confused because you do not command him."

"What the hell does that mean?"

"You must help him understand why these strangers are here. And you must help them by ordering this duende and the other spirits to leave them alone. But that is not all. You must gain Spirit Sky's confidence, then ask him where the tomb is of the evil one. We have got to find that tomb so that we can tell the archaeologists about it and then make sure the area around it gets sealed off permanently.

"Kan-Bah, how in the world am I supposed to do that?"

"Talk to him. Talk to him in the same language you use to communicate with Naja. The ancient tongue is called 'Pech', and you are one of the only people on earth that knows the language."

"Okay, assuming you are right, what am I supposed to say to this…this duende?"

"Talk to him as you would a supplicant. You will know what to say. Speak from your mind, but more importantly, speak from your heart. You must speak from your heart. And you must remember at all times, he does not see you as you are today. He still sees the ruler who wields jaguar claws. And to him, you are an absolute God. Your word is unquestioned final law. Your orders must be followed to the letter under penalty of death. And that is how you will get him to lead us to the forbidden tomb."

"Forbidden tomb," Brandon repeated. "I hope you people know I am not having a good time here! Forbidden frapping tomb. All I thought we were doing was giving this pissed off duende a taxi ride home. Now, here I am looking for a 'forbidden tomb'? And wait a minute, the downside is, if we screw up bad enough, it could possibly end the world. Have I got all that straight?"

"Yes, that's about the size of it," Didier chimed in. "But don't forget the part about you being the only person on the face of the earth that can pull it off," Didier looked around with an elfish grin. "The absolute *only one*! No pressure, understand!"

Brandon looked at Didier and shook his head. "Christ! And I have to be descended from this kind of 'heritage'? Anybody want to see my family photo album," He said to no one in particular. "Okay, whatever. Let's just do what we've got to do…what *I've* got to do, and then blow his pop stand as soon as possible. I hate to ruin the party, but did anybody hear me mention that I'm not having a good time?"

And so, they waited in that musty smelling inner chamber of the small pyramid. But they didn't have to wait long, for the duende responded to their presence and manifested itself before them as a green apparition, floating slightly above the ground. When it pivoted around enough to see Brandon, it fell onto its knees in supplication and again extended the scepter it held as if to hand it to the person he recognized at Ba'alam Ma'ax.

Brandon took a deep breath and said in a language that he and Naja had shared for years, "I am Jaguar Man. I have come here to tell you, these visitors among you have come in peace. They come here respectfully. They seek only to learn about the magnificent Maya who lived here, to learn about your wonderful accomplishments so they can go forth and tell others what honorable people you were. Leave them in peace. Kill no more visitors. This is my command to you, and all those who follow you. Now, rise. You are now the leader of this city. I am leaving you and my command to you is to lead these people with wisdom, but most of all, lead them in peace. Tell them to rest."

The duende looked at Brandon and seemed somewhat confused. But he stood erect, then bowed deeply as if he had understood.

"There is more," Brandon continued in the ancient language of Pech. "I must know the location of the place where the evil one who lived among you, rests. You must take me there."

The apparition looked frightened and confused.

"Do not worry," Brandon said. "My purpose is to warn the earth people to not disturb this area. But to warn them, I must know its location. I want you to show me, and to show him." Brandon gestured toward Kan-Bah.

Of course, no one understood a word Brandon had said. That is, except the duende and Kan-Bah, who seemed to understand perfectly. Kan-Bah said, "Good! You have done well, now let us leave this place and follow the duende to the forbidden tomb."

As they exited the small pyramid, Andrea asked," What did you say to that green thing, Brandon?"

"I told him, to quit fucking with people."

"Oh," she quipped. "Yeah, that's kind of what I thought you said. Do you think he understood?"

"According to Kan-Bah, he must have."

"That's some message to put to an ancient Maya spirit. 'Quit fucking with people.' Who would have thought it?"

Brandon turned to Kan-Bah. "Okay, I've done what you told me to do. Now what?"

"We wait here," Kan-Bah said. "We wait and see if Spirit Sky appears and leads us to the forbidden tomb."

"What would stop him?"

"Credibility. Whether you were believable and communicated well with him or not."

"Sonofabitch! Now I've got to stand here and wonder if I made a good impression on a ghost! I've gotta tell you, this has been one hell of a day."

Despite the pressure and seriousness of the moment, everyone laughed.

The small contingent didn't have to wait long to find out what Spirit Sky's response would be. A glow began to appear in the midst of them and finally took the shape of Spirit Sky. He stared directly at Brandon, then raised his left arm as if to point at something. A moment later, he started moving in the direction he had pointed.

Spirit Sky took his time and made it easy for the humans to follow him. They walked for almost a half hour before Spirit Sky stopped before a square platform only about six feet high that had a flat top, all made of carefully inlaid stone blocks. Surrounding the square platform on all four sides were stelae, each carved with hieroglyphics, which even to the unschooled eye seemed to depict evil. The carvings were of faces with fangs and evil looking eyes.

Now Spirit Sky pointed again, this time at the square platform. His look was foreboding. A moment later, he evaporated and was gone. Kan-Bah looked at the platform.

"Yes. This is it. I can feel the evil here. Somebody needs to go get every researcher, every scientist, every archaeologist and bring them here. The rest of us need to guard this place and allow nothing to disturb it. This place is what the other spirits have been afraid of, that researchers would find and excavate. That must never, *never* happen."

Lorenzo volunteered to make the trip. "I'll go," he said nervously. "Chingow! This place gives me the pinche' willies." Almost before anyone could respond to Lorenzo's offer, he was gone, moving at a fast pace toward the main camp.

Brandon called to his new jaguar, Cisco and commanded, "Go with the man and protect him from danger!" Cisco instantly responded, catching up with Lorenzo and kept pace with him.

"It's starting to turn to dusk," Didier said, looking around. "I hope Lorenzo gets back here quickly. I don't know about any of you, but I don't have a flashlight."

"I think he will be back quickly," Kan-Bah said. "Besides, we have a very protective jaguar here to take care of us."

"That's true," Didier said, then he called Naja to him.

Indeed, they did have two very protective jaguars guarding them. One by their side, and one flanking Lorenzo. Jaguars that seemed to be alert for any threat against their human family.

Sure enough, by the time dark was setting in, several flashlights could be seen approaching the small group watching over the platform. Lorenzo, slightly winded, still with Cisco by his side, rushed up to the group and said, "I traveled as fast as I could."

"We know, and thank you," Andrea said as Lorenzo handed her a flashlight.

Brad Harding stepped forward from the new arrivals. "Well, jolly. We're here. Now do you mind telling us why?"

"Do you want to get your problem solved with all these green poltergeists?" Brandon asked.

"Quite obviously, yes," Brad responded.

"Then listen up, everybody. And you had better listen good, because this is life or death important. Here's the way it is..." Brandon began a detailed explanation and summed it up by pointing out that the platform before them was most likely the epicenter of the problem, that under no circumstances was it to be excavated or molested in any way, forever and a day.

The group of learned archaeologists seemed to understand perfectly. "If you do this one thing," Brandon concluded, "these damned pesky ghosts will disappear and not bother you anymore. You will be able to continue your work in peace. But here's the down-side; *if* somebody, even one person, gets stupid and disturbs this platform or any of these stelae in any way. The consequences could be catastrophic. I recommend that you surround this thing with barbed wire and enough signs that a brain-dead idiot could figure it out. It would also not be a bad idea to contact the Honduran military and get an armed guard or two out here."

"Would they do that?" somebody asked.

"Well, they assign guards to protect other Maya sites located deep in the jungle, just to keep looters from coming in and digging into the tombs, looking for treasure. So, I think, yes, they would be willing to help you people out."

With that, Brandon and party received an enthusiastic round of applause. A couple of the researchers quickly marked the platform with cans of spray paint. Then, everybody was off, returning to the main camp.

This included Brandon and party. Everyone was happy, but

it had been a long day. Then, something odd happened. Kan-Bah paused en route back to the tent city set up by the researchers.

"What are you looking for?" Brandon asked. "If we leave by dawn, we can make it back to The Jungle Inn by early-afternoon, rest up and head for la Ceiba the next day. I'll buy you a plane ticket back to Guatemala and give you traveling money so you can buy a bus ticket to Chichicastenango."

"That won't be necessary," Kan-Bah said. My work is done there. This is where I am needed now."

"What does that mean? You aren't going back to the hotel with us?"

"No. I'm not even going back to the encampment with you. But thank you. I have enjoyed knowing you all. I must leave you, but I will remember you, Andrea, Lorenzo, Didier, Brandon, Naja, Cisco. You are all good souls."

Then Kan-Bah shook hands with everyone and turned to walk back the way they had come. But after he had walked several feet away, the spirit walker began to fade and then was gone, disappeared, evaporated before their eyes. And that is the last they saw of Kan-Bah.

Lorenzo said, "Hijo de la chingada! The Viejo was a ghost all along?"

"Yes. A real shaman, it would seem," Brandon answered.

Lorenzo continued staring in the direction where Kan-Bah had evaporated. "He didn't seem like no pinche' ghost. He was sitting right beside me in the truck for hours. We were talking and everything. He drank beer with me Chingow! A fucking fantasma, right beside me, and I never knew it!"

Perhaps because of the trip, or perhaps because of the stress of the events of the evening, everyone in 'The Brandon Shaw Party' suddenly felt weary as they walked the rest of the way back to the researcher's tent city.

When they got there, Brandon walked up to the people

who had not been present at the platform and announced, "Tell your co-workers, researchers, archaeologists, whatever, that I don't think they will be hounded by the green things anymore. Your co-workers need to explain 'the forbidden platform' to you. From now on, you can continue with your work, unafraid and unbothered, like normal people."

"How can we be sure?" Brad said, with one hand on his side.

"Just call it a hunch," Brandon answered. Then, "Listen, it's been a long day. And that trip across from the Jungle Inn has worn us out a little more than I thought. You wouldn't by any chance have a spare tent around here, would you?"

"Certainly, we have two. The one Sam abandoned in such a hurry, and the one belonging to Bruce, who went to check on Sam. He did say he would be back at some point."

"I'm sure he will," Brandon said. "He's just been delayed with a side trip for a few days."

"Bully!" Brad said. "I'll show you where the tents are. Then, if you would like showers, we have that set up."

"Showers?" Andrea said with obvious delight.

"Certainly. No shortage of water in the jungle. It's just a matter of heating it, you see. But nothing a little ingenuity can't solve. We have a solar water heater set up. It's a tank painted black, so it absorbs heat from the sun. I think you'll find it quite accommodating." Brad showed his guests where the facilities were, then said, "I really must go explain what's going on to my companions. I want to thank you, for whatever switch it is that you have flipped. By the way, where is the short, Maya looking chap?"

"Oh, he's around," Andrea said with a knowing smile.

"Very well then," Brad said with finality. "I'm off. Might see you around the campfire tonight for supper, eh what?"

"We'll be there," Brandon assured him.

After moving things from the vehicles, into tents; Brandon

and Andrea, taking Sam's tent, Lorenzo and Didier taking Bruce's tent; Brandon and Andrea went to check out the shower arrangement.

Andrea giggled with relief and delight when she saw the creative ingenuity of the archaeologists. They had set up a rather large shower using blue plastic tarps for the four walls. They had rigged a makeshift water cistern above the shower with a genuine showerhead. The water was indeed warmed by the sun. The floor of the shower was a large, flat piece of limestone that had either previously been there, or they moved in place.

She and Brandon enjoyed a long bath together, each washing the other's back, among other things. At least, the back is where it started. But then Brandon wrapped Andrea in his arms, reached around her and took her full breasts in his hands, working the soap with sensuous pleasure. It only took Andrea moments to respond to Brandon's touch.

She turned so that she was facing him, put her arms around his neck and kissed him deeply, passionately. Then she turned loose of his neck and dropped her hands down until she found what she was looking for.

Back at the main part of the encampment, Lorenzo either suspected what Brandon and Andrea were up to or thought it likely could happen. In either case, he retrieved his CD player/boom box from the truck and put on some tipico Hondureno music to serve as a sound block.

Andrea giggled when she heard the music drifting toward them from two hundred feet away, because she knew exactly what Lorenzo was doing. And she took full advantage of Lorenzo's gift. She moaned with rapture as she guided Brandon into her and rode him, there in the shower, for a long overdue moment of tender passion.

As always, a deep feeling of security and love swept over her as she approached her magic moment. Then, it was upon her and she completely surrendered herself, melted in Brandon's arms. Likewise, Brandon held this incredible woman to him as he reached a tumultuous orgasm.

When he recovered his breath enough, he gently held Andrea's face in his hands, looked her in the eyes and said, "I'll tell you a secret. All my life I have wanted to be totally loved by an awesome woman. But I never thought it was going to happen. I put it in the category of a fantasy. But you're real! You are real, and you're here, and you are more than I ever dreamed of. I want you to know that. I want you to know you are the beat of my heart, and the keeper of my dreams. You are one awesome woman, Andrea Granger. And I vow to you two things. One, I will love you forever. Two, I will never take you for granted. Not for a second."

Andrea smiled at her man, then kissed him again, deeply, passionately.

———

That night, there was a large gathering around a very bright campfire. Brandon and Andrea were introduced around, and then Brandon was asked to repeat his announcement about the retreat of the Maya spirits. He was probed, or at least several people tried, to get him to say how he knew this; but Brandon kept close counsel except to say, "Your friend Brad can answer most of your questions. Get him to explain about the square platform, but not tonight. Tonight, let's breathe a sigh of relief and enjoy ourselves. For now, it's enough to know you are safe, at least from the hadas (spirits), and can continue your work here in peace."

Brandon tried to follow his own advice and relax. But something else was bothering him. Sitting close by his side, Andrea could feel her man's apprehension. He would keep it inside for now, but she knew that whatever it was would have to bubble to the surface sooner or later. It would be mandatory that when it did, she had to be there for him. For this, if no other reason, she stuck with him like glue.

Somebody broke out steaks and knew what they were doing when it came to cooking over an open fire. It was a pleasant evening except for one thing. Andrea noticed that Lorenzo was nursing a bottle of Flor De Cana rum pretty hard. He didn't let up and as the evening aged, Lorenzo wound up in the bag.

The ever observant Didier commented, "Something is bothering Lorenzo. I know him pretty well and I've never seen him do this."

"I know," Andrea agreed. "I wonder what it is?"

That night, Andrea slept on the cot in the tent. Brandon made a pallet and slept on the nylon tent floor, sandwiched between two jaguars. The night was alive with the sounds of tree frogs and hundreds of other nocturnal creatures. It was a relaxing symphony.

The next morning, Lorenzo, looking rough from the night before, recruited some men to help him offload the home-made sarcophagus. There was no continued use for it now that the duende had been returned to its home. This would make the truck several hundred pounds lighter and improve the odds of it not getting stuck on the return trip.

Of course, there was a great deal of curiosity about the home-made sarcophagus, and explanations were hard to come by, because nobody was going to believe the truth. So, Lorenzo just said that Brandon would explain it, and then Brandon pretended to be far too busy to 'get into it'.

After wishing all their new friends a heart-felt goodbye and good health, the Brandon Shaw Party mounted up for the return trip through the forest to The Jungle Inn. But this time, Didier decided to ride in the truck with Lorenzo. Not only was the back seat of the Jeep crowded with Naja and Cisco, but Didier secretly had something else on his mind. Being the caring person he was, it was his plan to gently probe and try to find out what was eating at Lorenzo.

The main thing he was subjected to, however, was a lot of gear jamming as Lorenzo negotiated the old truck around the hundreds of curves to avoid trees. The slight Amer-Indian also groaned a lot, a side effect of his aching head, and at one point, Lorenzo had to stop the truck and get out for a breath of fresh air.

This was accompanied with a mumbling of "Hijole' Chingow! Duele la pinche cabeza!"

The problem was this time he didn't have the magic hand of Kan-Bah to relieve his pain. He would have to ride it out to the end, and it was a rough ride!

"Kind of got carried away last night, eh?" Didier said, trying to make it sound off-hand.

"Yeah. Didn't mean to. But you know; the beautiful campfire, the night, the stars, the jungle, everybody having a good time talking. It was nice. I just got carried away. Bueno, plus I guess I've just got a lot of shit on my mind." Lorenzo swerved to miss a large branch hanging out into the road.

"Hmm. Interesting," Didier said. "Want to talk about it?"

"Not especially," Lorenzo said. "Nothing to talk about." And then, several minutes later, "Wouldn't do no good anyway."

Didier looked over at Lorenzo. "Sometimes just talking about something helps, even if it doesn't actually solve the problem."

Lorenzo drove for a few minutes more without saying anything. Then, "I like you, Señor Didier. You a really good person and you have always treated me with respect. But if I tell you what's bugging me, you promise to keep it just between us?"

"Of course," Didier said truthfully.

"Bueno. Sabes que, when Don Brandon decided to move to

the United States, he turned Jungle Cargo over to me and the girls. Legally, we're the owners of Jungle Cargo."

"Okay. I didn't know that, but it doesn't surprise me. Brandon is a very generous person. He has a good heart. And besides, it was a wise decision. Who else knows that compound and the business better than you?"

"Si. Yeah, yeah… Perhaps this is true. Maybe it's even part of the problem."

"What do you mean?"

"Well, the truth is, Jungle Cargo just isn't the same without him being around. I been working for him since I was a pinche' kid, you know? He like, raised me. But now, with him being in Florida, I walk out on that big deck in the morning where we used to have such great meetings, and it's just… I keep looking around, hoping he'll be there, sitting at that table, eating mango, Naja by his side, and yes, Andrea too. But…he ain't there and the whole thing just has no meaning. I have lost my reason why. Does that make sense?"

Didier smiled knowingly. "I understand *exactly* what you're saying."

"Having him down here has been great. But now, this pinche' 'mission' is almost complete. This is almost over. He, Naja, Andrea, and now I imagine even Cisco will be leaving again, para pinche' Florida."

"So, you miss him?"

"Yeah, I miss him. I miss him a lot. I'm not sure why. He can be a royal pain in the ass most of the time. But… He's closer to me than my own father ever was."

"Well, what are you going to do about it?"

"Hijo! I don't know. That's just it. I don't know what I can do."

"Simple. Talk to him about it."

"'Simple?' Mira! Sabes que, nothing is ever that goddamn

simple with Brandon Shaw. Chingow! I thought you knew him, Didier."

"I know him well enough to know that he misses Jungle Cargo, and you are a part of Jungle Cargo."

"You think so? How you know that?"

"Lorenzo, mi amigo. I thought you knew me!"

Lorenzo glanced over at Didier, then back at the road, and smiled. "You know, you are one smart mother fucker, Amigo. I'm glad that I know you.

———

The return trip through the jungle, although arduous was uneventful. By the time the two-vehicle convoy pulled up in front of the Jungle Inn, everybody was exhausted, spent, wanted nothing more than a bath and a bed. Supper didn't even have any appeal, although they did accept drinks from behind the bar to help chase away the misery.

In truth, it was barely past noon. But the twisting and turning journey through the Mosquitia Jungle had seemed like an all-day affair, and justifiably so, for with each turn, the body must adjust to the change in gravity and compensate. Besides, the safari to The Lost City of The Monkey God had been emotionally draining on several levels.

The one factor alone, the revelation by Brandon Shaw that indeed he may be the descendant of Jaguar Man was enough to leave anyone's head spinning. Then there was the "evaporation" of Kan-Bah. The meeting, face to face with the restless duende! What else could they possibly have to deal with?

For now, both Naja and Cisco were hungry, and their needs had to be met. Luckily, Pedro, Didier's Concierge, bartender, waiter and general manager (unofficial) as it were, had foreseen this problem and made sure it was planned for. Two fresh tapir legs were brought out and presented to the cats. They would take their time eating and then most likely take advantage of the water trough.

Andrea was a little surprised when Brandon plopped down in one of the rattan chairs in the bar instead of going to their room. After watching him for a minute, she decided to join him at the table and find out what was going on.

"Something's bothering you. What is it?"

Brandon hesitated for several long moments. Andrea patiently waited. Finally, "I…that vision… If, and I repeat, *if* that was really me. I was a cold-blooded mass murderer. If Kan-Bah had to take me down some prehistoric memory lane, why the hell did he choose that particular memory, or vision, or whatever the bleeding hell it was?"

"First of all, I'm not sure the choice was his," Andrea said. "He probably had no control over what you would see."

Didier showed up at the table with a tall drink and joined them in mid-conversation. But he had no trouble catching up.

"Second of all," Andrea continued," what you saw happened approximately two thousand years ago. The value of life as opposed to death was completely different. There's no way to judge the morality of it using twenty-first century standards. But okay, let's say for just a second that you do. Look what you're doing to yourself. You're wringing yourself out, torturing yourself because of what you know is right and wrong. That should tell you something, something very important."

"What?" Brandon asked, looking at his drink.

At this point, Didier interrupted. "Quite simply, you have a very strong conscience, my old friend; a moral compass to guide you on the path of doing the right thing. There is nothing left of you that is like the former, ancient 'you', with the exception perhaps of your unusual ability to communicate with animals, which I see as a blessing. I saw how you suffered when Naja was missing and you didn't know whether she was injured or not. People who are cold, who 'don't feel' do not behave the way you did."

"Do you understand?" Andrea asked.

Brandon looked at her, although his head was still lowered.

Slightly exasperated, Andrea said, "Okay, let me put it another way. Never in my life have I heard of someone having their panties in a twist over something that may or may not have happened two fucking thousand years ago. Enough of this bullshit. I'm going to take a bath and then to bed. Goodnight, all." With that, she retreated toward their room with a stride that indicated she was slightly perturbed.

Brandon looked at Didier. "She makes a good point."

"A damn good point!" Didier said, smiling, as he lifted his glass to his lips to take a sip.

"Well, fuck this," Brandon said, rising from his chair and following Andrea. "I'm gonna go take a shower too…so I can see her *naked*! Wait up!" he called to his woman as he rushed down the corridor.

CHAPTER SEVEN

A Fond Farewell

AFTER A GOOD BREAKFAST AND FOND FAREWELL, THE JUNGLE Cargo contingent bade Didier goodbye and set out toward the west, back the way they had come. Nobody was looking forward to the slow, tortuous grinding crawl over the network of roots that made up the road/tunnel through the jungle on the way out, but there was no avoiding it. So, the best thing to do was take a deep breath, bite down on a rag and dig in.

Six hours later, when they emerged from the seeming endless green tunnel, everyone in both vehicles breathed a deep sigh of relief. This was the first long trip Cisco had ever taken in a vehicle, and he seemed slightly apprehensive about the constant movement. So, Brandon made the decision to pull over and let everyone stretch their legs, especially the cats.

Cisco had been riding with Lorenzo, but because of his nervous state, Brandon decided to move him into the back seat of the Jeep with Naja. It would be crowded, but the cats didn't seem to mind, especially here. The road, while not perfect wouldn't be as jarring as inside the tunnel. Therefore, the cats could assume a sitting position, look around and be diverted by the passing scenery. This way, they would be quite content.

Two hours farther down the road, Andrea read a sign announcing that Trujillo was just ahead. "When we get to the Trujillo cut-off," she said, "turn right. I want to go to Sad Mary's."

"What on earth for?" Brandon asked.

"There's something I want to do," she answered with a slightly coy smile.

Brandon knew it would do no good to push her, so he returned his gaze to the road ahead and drove. At one point he picked up the walkie talkie to talk to Lorenzo.

"Hey, we're gonna pull into Trujillo for a minute. Andrea wants to go to Sad Mary's"

"What for?" came the voice over the walkie talkie.

"Nobody knows!" Brandon said. "And there's no use asking."

Thirty minutes later, the two-vehicle convoy pulled over to the curb in front of Sad Mary's Cafe. Everybody got out, including the two jaguars and went inside. Sad Mary was standing close to the back of the dining room. She looked up when the contingent entered.

"Well, kiss my ass! I'm surprised to see you people. Don't get me wrong. I'm happy to see you, just, what the hell are you doing here? Oh look! You've got two jaguars now! Where did the other one come from?"

Andrea walked up to Sad Mary, smiling. "Sad Mary, you need a vacation.

"Whaaaat? What the hell are you talking about?"

"I'm inviting you to pack a bag and come with us, right now, to Cuyamel. Spend a few days on the beach."

"Are you out of your mind? I've got a business to run."

"How long has Marta been working for you?"

"Hell, I don't know. For years I suppose."

"Yes, and she probably knows more about how to run this place better than you do."

Sad Mary shook her head. "I can't argue with that. But…"

"Let Marta run this place for a week or two. I'd be willing to bet that when you come back here, she'll have everything in better shape than it is now, with you in the way all of the time. When is the last time you took some time off?"

"Well now, let me think…how about, *never*."

"I'm offering you a chance to get away for a few days and enjoy life while you still can. Do something for *you*. We have a pretty good-sized house at Cuyamel. We have a guest room just for you. This is the opportunity of a lifetime for you. Trust me, take it!"

Sad Mary looked deep into Andrea's eyes. Finally, a smile came to her lips and she said, "By God! I'm gonna do it! I might be crazy. Hell, people think I am anyway. I'm gonna go with you. Just give me a few minutes to pack a few things."

"Where do you live?" Andrea asked.

"Upstairs."

"Okay. While you do that, I'll explain what's going on to Marta, and let's get the hell out of Dodge as quickly as possible. Cuyamel is waiting."

"I'm already gone," Mary said as she headed for the stairs in the back of the building.

Less than half an hour later, Sad Mary was climbing into the back seat of the Jeep. For this leg of the trip, the two jaguars had to be moved back to the truck with Lorenzo. He didn't seem to mind. It would give him somebody to talk to, even if they didn't understand. Besides, it seemed that a special bond was forming between him and Cisco.

Andrea and Mary chatted like school-girls as the convoy made its way along the road. Three hours later, they pulled up in front of Jungle Cargo. The long journey was at its conclusion.

Exhaustion was the order of the day. The two jaguars were fed and offered the run if they wanted to stay there. Sad Mary was introduced to Anna Maria and Suyapa, then shown to a guest room where she would be the honored guest of the house for the next week or so. Brandon and Andrea headed for the shower.

As they got undressed, Brandon said, " Okay, are you going to keep me in the dark about what's up your sleeve with Sad Mary, or am I just supposed to watch the movie and follow along?"

"Watch the movie," Andrea said. "The plot will become clear in less time than you think."

CHAPTER EIGHT

The Transformation

IT SEEMED LIKE THEY HAD JUST CLOSED THEIR EYES WHEN Brandon and Andrea heard the sounds of the girls in the kitchen preparing breakfast. They sounded particularly happy and excited, apparently elated that everyone had returned from the mission healthy and happy.

Coffee was the main fuel to bring everyone back to life who had been on the arduous trip. They made their way out onto the deck, plopped in chairs around the round table and sat sipping, but saying little.

From far down the beach, although it was early in the morning, stone cutting saws could be heard quarrying the limestone needed for Don Houseman's new house. He knew about the force of hurricane's and also knew this location was in the direct path of Hurricane Alley. Therefore, he determined that if a hurricane was going to take his house, it was damn well going to have to work for it.

His house would rise from a poured concrete slab, but it would still be a beach-house, fourteen feet off of the ground. Stone arches would reach from ground to floor level, but the walls would also be thick limestone. The house would be sixteen hundred square feet and feature mahogany floors, plus a huge deck would stretch away from the front of the house toward the Caribbean. Don Houseman knew his business.

Sad Mary made her appearance on the front deck to join her friends. Cheerful morning greetings were offered.

"How does it feel to be on vacation?" Andrea asked, over the top of her coffee cup.

Sad Mary looked around and shook her head. "Like I'm dreaming," she said rather softly, and very unlike the loud and brash Sad Mary of Trujillo.

"I swear, I'm scared that if I blink, I'm going to wake up and be shoveling yuca into a pot to make slop for the heathen seamen that infest Trujillo."

Everybody sitting at the table chuckled.

"Well, get a good breakfast in you. You and I have a busy day."

"Busy day? What do you mean?"

"I mean, you and I are going to La Ceiba this morning, just as soon as you can eat and get ready.

"La Ceiba! Well, that would be nice, but what for? I mean, any special reason?

"Yep," Andrea said mischievously. "It's a surprise, so I'm not telling why."

A little while later, as Andrea steered Sad Mary through the house toward the back steps and toward the Jeep, Andrea stopped long enough to peck Brandon on the cheek and leave bright red lipstick marks.

"We'll be back," she said. Then she stopped, walked back to Brandon and whispered, "Ask Don Housman to join us for dinner tonight." Then she winked as she turned away.

"Well, you little minx!" Brandon said. "Are you planning what I think you're planning?"

"I'll never tell," Andrea said, and was out the back door, following Sad Mary down the steps.

As the Jeep drove away, Brandon returned to the deck to have a meeting with Lorenzo. The two men got fresh cups of coffee, settled down at the table. By now, two curious jaguars also joined the group. Brandon scratched Naja's ears, Lorenzo did the same for Cisco, who was continuing to bond very strongly with Lorenzo.

Brandon began to talk. "Okay, we've dealt with the damned duende. The sonofabitch is gone, gone, gone and good riddance. So now it's time to start turning things around and trying to get back to normal at this compound. I want you to get in the truck and make a milk run to these little villages around here. Spread the word that the fucking hada is no more. We need those Indians to start bringing parrots here or we've got big trouble."

Doug arrived at that moment and joined the men at the table, coffee cup in hand.

"Yep," Doug said. "And that doesn't mean just uh, this end. I'm in trouble too if I uh, I don't, don't have any stock to sell in Florida. This uh, uh, ghost thing has really put us in a bind. Hell, thrown a monkey wrench into the works. You know these Indians, Lorenzo. We're depending on you. You are our key."

"You da man wid da plan," Brandon said with a smile.

Lorenzo nodded agreement. "Okay, Jefe. I'll make the rounds and talk to as many people as I can."

"Tell you what. I'm gonna call Andrea and have her bring us a hundred, pint sized bottles of Flor De Cana rum. You put the word out that the first hundred hunters who show up here with parrots get a free bottle of rum. That ought to get the wheels turning."

"Hijole'!" Lorenzo said with abroad smile. "You sure know how to start a fire!"

The men laughed and Lorenzo bounded down the steps, a

happy gait to his walk. Before he could get sidetracked doing something else, Brandon called Andrea on her cell phone.

"Yes, dear?" she said when she answered.

"I know this is going to sound strange, but while you're in town, go to the liquor store and get me 100 pint sized bottles of Flor De Cana. Also, pick up stuff for a big party here this weekend."

"I had already planned on supplies for a party," she said. "The one hundred bottles of rum tells me you're up to something. I won't ask, at least not until I get home."

Meanwhile, Brandon and Doug decided to take a walk down the beach and see what kind of progress Don Houseman was making. They had to go in any case, so as to invite Don to dinner. Naja accompanied them. Cisco had apparently joined Lorenzo in making his milk-run announcement. The day was taking shape nicely, and Brandon was happy normalcy was returning to his realm.

By late afternoon, Brandon, Doug and Don were sitting at the table on the deck, sipping ice cold beer and chatting. Naja was at Brandon's side, panting in the heat. There was easy laughter when suddenly Brandon's ears perked because he thought he heard the sound of the Jeep coming through the entranceway.

Indeed, it was. A moment later, Jeep doors slammed, and the sound of footsteps could be heard coming up the back stairs. A few moments later, Andrea emerged through the patio doors followed by an attractive woman whom Brandon did not recognize, at least not at first.

When he did recognize her, his jaw dropped, and he pushed his way up out of his chair. The two women crossed the deck, stopping in front of him.

"Honey," Andrea said, I'd like to introduce you to Mary Thompson."

Brandon was in mild shock. Standing there, looking

somewhat stunning, was a woman who, although she was past her prime, was still quite beautiful, poised and demure, dressed in a peach colored sun dress with a full skirt. She was properly accessorized with matching low heel shoes, necklace, a bracelet and earrings.

Mouth agape, Brandon extended his hand. "Sad Mary? Is that you? I, I can't believe it!"

"Sad Mary died," Mary said. "We left Sad Mary in Trujillo. And I want a hug, not a handshake." Mary stepped forward and gave Brandon a very lady-like hug.

Still in shock, Brandon indicated Don Houseman. "Mary, I'd like to introduce you to Don Houseman. Don is our new neighbor. He's building a house down the beach a way."

"Oh?" Mary said, shaking Don's hand. "What kind of house is it?"

"It's going to be a beach house," Don answered. But I'm using a lot of on-site natural resources, limestone, for the arches and walls."

"Really?" Mary said. I'd love to see it sometime."

"Well," Don said with a smile, "I'd be honored. Actually, we aren't very far along on construction, but yes, I'd love to show it to you."

Brandon pulled Andrea to one side as the conversation progressed between Don Houseman and Mary. "What in the world did you do? Put her through a time machine? Good grief, I hardly recognized her when you two stepped through that door."

"It's amazing what a little TLC can do," Andrea said with a smile. "Plus, a makeover. I got her hair done, nails, makeup, tried to restore some of her self-worth and dignity, to say nothing of self-confidence, pep talked her a bit. New dress. Things like that."

"Well, my love, you are a freaking miracle worker. Maybe I should say, miracle worker *again*! As far as I'm concerned, it's another reason to love you. I mean, look at her! You've saved her life, certainly from an existence of misery and despair. So, this is what you had in mind all along? For her to meet Don Houseman?"

"Yes, but first, she had to be ready to meet Don Houseman or it wouldn't have worked. I had to get her in the right frame of mind, and that meant restoring hope by restoring belief in herself. I had to prove to her that she still has it."

"Obviously she does. Who would have thought?" They looked over at the developing conversation between Don and Mary, who were now sitting in chairs at the table.

"Looks like it's going pretty well," Andrea said.

"Amazing!" Brandon said. "Just frapping amazing. I am so proud of you. Well, I think we should give them space and keep our fingers crossed."

"That's the plan," Andrea said, as she took Brandon's hand and led him inside the house.

It was at that moment that Brandon's cell phone rang. He answered.

"Hello? Yeah, this is Brandon Shaw… Well, not that it's any of your business, but we have two cats, Naja and Cisco. Why do you ask? Well, they prefer tapir legs… Tapir. Tapir, you know, as in, an animal that looks a little like a rhino with a nose like a short elephant's trunk. They really like it better when they can go hunting and kill fresh ones, but that isn't always possible. Hello? You still there? … Well, we usually get them from the Indians around here. They shoot them and bring them to us… Oh, yes… No, they like the whole leg, bone and all. They crunch the bone into fine pieces. The calcium is good for them. Of course, the thing they like even better than tapir, is when they can get their paws on some asshole tele-marketer. The only bad part is, by the time we squeeze the bullshit out of them, there isn't that much left… Hello? Hello?"

Brandon looked at Andrea. "Well! He hung up on me! That was rude."

Andrea laughed. "Maybe it was something you said."

"Nah, couldn't have been that. All I did was answer his dumb questions."

Lorenzo returned from his milk run. He came into the house, a little tired but looking satisfied. He headed directly to the fridge for a beer.

"Okay, I talked to all the Indians around here. The word ought to spread like a brush fire. You know these pinche' Indians. They don't seem to have anything better to do than sit around gossiping like a bunch of old women."

"Look out!" Andrea said, teasingly.

No disrespect," Lorenzo said, as he plopped down in a bar stool next to the kitchen island. "Besides, you aren't old, Doña. You are young and beautiful."

"Good save!" she said.

"Oh! Mira! I sweetened the pot a little with the Indians," Lorenzo said.

"What do you mean?" Brandon asked.

"Bueno, I told them that whoever brought us the most baby parrots this coming month would win not one but two brand new machetes with scabbards."

Brandon laughed. "That's pure genius. Good job, my man."

"No problem," Lorenzo said, then he looked out on the deck and saw the conversation at the table.

"Speaking of women, who is the new dama elegante out there talking with Don?

Brandon and Andrea looked at each other, and laughed, knowingly.

"Come with me, Lorenzo," Andrea said. You should meet the new 'dama elegante'. I think you'll like her."

With that, Lorenzo, led by Andrea, and followed by

Brandon, and the two jaguars, departed through the patio doors onto the deck and crossed to the table. It was obvious that Lorenzo's curiosity was peaked.

As the trio neared the table, Don looked up. Mary's back was toward the house, so her face was hidden.

"Well, hi there," Don said, as he rose from the table. "Did your errand go well?"

"Sure did," Lorenzo answered Don, but he was looking at the back of the lady seated at the table.

"I'm assuming you know Mary Thompson?" Don said, indicating Mary.

It was at this point that Mary stood up and turned. "Hello Lorenzo," Mary said pleasantly.

"Hi," Lorenzo said, extending his hand in greeting. "I, listen, please forgive me. It seems like I should know you. But, mucho gusto. I am very happy to meet you. Bienvenidos to this house."

"You don't have to be so formal with me, you young whipper snapper!" Mary said with a coy smile.

For several moments, Lorenzo was dead silent as he stared at Mary. Finally, the dawn!

"Sad Mary? No. You can't be Sad Mary. I mean, hijole' you look a little bit like her, but…what's going on here?"

"To begin with," Andrea said. "It's not 'Sad' Mary anymore. We buried Sad Mary in Trujillo. This is Mary Thompson from Atlanta."

Lorenzo continued to stare, squinting his eyes, eventually shaking his head. "My God! I don't believe it. It really is you, isn't it? I mean, it's you, but it's not you. Shit! I don't know what I mean. I am totally confused. What happened to you? You look *great*! More than great. You, you look like a new person!"

"Thank you, Lorenzo. I feel like one too, thanks to our wonderful Andrea."

Lorenzo sank into a chair. If somebody had told me about this, I wouldn't have believed them. I mean, I'm looking straight at Mary, you are a beautiful woman.

How—"

"Lorenzo," Andrea interrupted, "Come with us back into the house. I'll tell you all about it. I promise. Meanwhile, we're interrupting Don and Mary's conversation."

Andrea took Lorenzo by the hand and pulled him out of the chair, toward the patio doors. He was speechless as he continued to stare at the amazing transformation of Sad Mary into Mary Thompson.

"It looks like you've launched a beautiful ship," Brandon said, as Andrea and Lorenzo came through the patio doors into the house.

"Yes," Andrea said, as she looked out on the deck at the couple in conversation. "May she swim well."

———

Brandon fired up the barbeque pit that evening and grilled steaks. Each steak was cooked to order, depending on how the individual preferred their meat. Brandon considered himself something of a perfectionist when cooking over an open fire. In the kitchen where he had total control over the heat level, he was at a loss. But here, where a little bit of cave man and danger was required, he was in his realm.

After a very pleasant dinner and conversation, the party splintered. Don invited Mary to walk down the beach with him so he could show her his house, under construction. The girls had dishes to wash, and the jaguars wanted to wander around in the brush behind the compound.

Brandon was a little alarmed to see that Lorenzo was once again drinking himself into a blob. Lorenzo stood at the railing of the deck, looking out at the water. He wasn't being loud or obnoxious, just getting sloppy drunk, and it was beginning to worry Brandon. He motioned for Andrea to join him, and they walked to the railing where they flanked Lorenzo.

"Okay," Brandon said. "You know I am not one to pussy-foot around. It's time we had a talk."

Lorenzo turned his beer up for a deep sip, but said nothing.

Brandon turned and leaned his rump against the railing, then crossed his arms.

"You may as well spit it out, Lorenzo, or I'm going to stand here all night. And truth told, I believe, in your heart, that you do want to talk. Tell Andrea and me what's on your mind."

After a few more moments and a deep sigh, Lorenzo looked down at the sand below them and said, "When you two aren't here, I miss you."

Brandon looked over at Andrea. "Well, I guess the truth is, we miss you too. But I don't know what we're supposed to do about it. We live in Florida now, and all of my work is in Florida."

"I know, I know," Lorenzo said in a defeated voice.

Andrea subtly motioned to Brandon to meet her inside. Both Brandon and Andrea patted Lorenzo on the shoulders, then retreated.

Once inside the house, Andrea said, "Lorenzo is really hurting. You can hear it in his voice, see it in his body language.

"I know," Brandon said. "But what are we supposed to do?"

"I don't know. But it's clear, we have got to figure something out."

"Well, you figure it out then. You are the only problem solver in this family. All I know how to do is screw up and make things worse."

With that, Brandon opened the patio door and rejoined Lorenzo on the deck. For starters, they would get plowed together and commiserate. Andrea watched them for a minute. She knew instinctively that although this appeared on the surface to just be one more small bump in the road, that was not the case at all.

Lorenzo had been Brandon's right hand man from the time he was a kid. When Brandon first purchased the property at Cuyamel, there had been nothing here but coconut trees. Lorenzo was there, working side by side with Brandon to clear the land and build this house. The same house where Andrea was standing this very second.

Lorenzo learned all there was to know about running this animal compound to the point that he was more than Brandon's manager. He was like the son that Brandon never had. And now, that son was hurting inside. It was a problem that could not be brushed aside as if it were hoity toity. It must be addressed, decisively and quickly.

The elephant in the room was that she and Brandon were now living in Florida. They had a whole new life there, and a successful business, based on Brandon making personal appearances and talking to groups of learned people about the jungle and the animals therein. His efforts had resulted in some positive actions being taken to stop deforestation of many of the world's jungles and reverse the destruction by getting tree planting started.

Brandon finally felt good about himself. He wouldn't stop his work, and Andrea certainly wouldn't want him to. So, how to maintain and continue that work, and at the same time deal with this problem? That, dear Hamlet, was the question.

As a sidebar, Andrea noticed, later that night, that the hour was getting late and Mary had not returned from 'down the beach' with Don Houseman.

"Well!" Andrea thought with a smile. "That little plan certainly went as hoped."

Now, if she could devise one as effective for Lorenzo. It was approaching the witching hour. Brandon and Lorenzo were sitting at the round table on the deck solving every problem in the world except the obvious one. Andrea yawned. She was tired. She would have to leave the two men on the deck to their own devices. It was bedtime.

CHAPTER NINE

Bad Ending To A Good Day

BREAKFAST WAS BEING PREPARED AND PLACED ATOP TABLES ON the front deck when Don Houseman and Mary Thompson made their appearance, chatting and laughing as they made their way up the staircase to the deck. Don carried a large Tupperware container with more of his delicious, deviled eggs.

Morning hellos were happily exchanged as the pair made their arrival. Don now seemed happy. Gone was the sadness in his eyes. As for Mary, she hardly looked like the wretched café owner from Sambala. 'That' woman was no more. In her place, Mary Thompson had emerged, vibrant and with sparkling eyes.

"You know," Mary owns a café in Trujillo," Don began. "Well of course you know. What am I saying? Anyway, I love to cook, so she's going to teach me some of her best recipes."

Andrea looked at Don, then over at Mary who was now walking toward her. Mary put her arms around Andrea and gave her a warm hug.

"You, you are a miracle worker," Mary said, happy but close to tears. "I don't know how to thank you. Andrea, you restored me. You gave me my life back."

"No, you did that," Andrea said, as she returned Mary's hug. "What I did was open a door you hadn't noticed. But you are the one who walked through that door, on your on."

"We both know there was more to it than that," Mary said, as she stepped back slightly. "I am so grateful. I will be forever grateful."

Andrea smiled. Mary retreated, and rejoined Don, sitting beside him.

Now, Andrea thought, if she could just pull one more rabbit out of the hat, the day would be complete.

Lorenzo emerged from the house, looking like it had been a very long night.

"Where is Kan-Bah?" he said. "I need him for my head."

"Me too!" Brandon said, as he came through the patio doors attired in his usual khaki shorts and safari shirt, a uniform that had been a part of him since before Andrea had known him. "They need a hangover filter for that damned Flor De Caña."

After Brandon got his coffee and his morning kiss from Andrea, he chose a chair and settled in at the table.

Don posed a question to him. "Brandon, I need a favor," Don said.

Brandon looked at the elderly gentleman. "What's that?"

"Mary and I would like to borrow your blue truck for the day. Well, actually, all day."

Brandon glanced at Andrea, then Lorenzo. "You know how to drive that thing? It's standard shift, you know."

Don laughed. "Brandon, when I was young, automatic transmissions were just coming on the market. Hell, I learned how to drive in an old 1949 Studebaker. Black with a grey interior. Worst car ever made. There was always something wrong with it, always."

"Sure. I don't mind loaning you the truck, but what are you going to do with it?"

Don looked at Mary and started to answer Brandon's question. But Mary jumped in.

"We're going to Trujillo," Mary said with a demure smile.

"Trujillo? The shit hole of the world? What for?" Brandon smiled, looked over at Andrea, who was already smiling and walking toward them with her coffee cup in hand.

"I'm going to turn the café over to Marta," Mary said with a smile. "I need to pack my personal belongings and, well, I'm coming back here with Don. We want to try to build a life together."

"Damn!" Brandon said. "That's awfully quick."

"When you're our age," Don said with a smile, "you don't have time to waste on indecision."

Then, there were congratulations, and everyone stood up for hugs, plus some back slapping among the men. Even Lorenzo got in on the act.

"If you would like, I could come along and be your driver," Lorenzo offered.

"Thanks, anyway," Don replied. "But it looks to me like you're going to have your hands full here."

"What do you mean?" Lorenzo asked.

"Maybe you need to take a walk to the other side of the house and peek out into the compound. Your PR milk-run the other day was effective."

Lorenzo walked through the house to the back door and looked out. At least a dozen Indians were there in the compound, patiently waiting on him, all carrying small home-made cages containing parrots.

"Hijole'!" he said. Then he hollered to the Indians to be patient, that he would be there as soon as possible. After that, he returned to the front deck.

"Duty calls," he said. "I'm not even going to get to eat breakfast." Then he took a deep sip of his coffee, grabbed a piece of pan dulce, and tromped down the side stairs by the deck.

"So, what's the deal?" Brandon asked Mary. "Are you just going to have Marta keep the café going, or what?"

"I'm going to do something similar to what you did with Lorenzo," Mary said. "I guess Marta is my Lorenzo. I'm just going to give her the whole shebang. She can run it, sell it, close it, whatever she wants to do. Thanks to Andrea, and now this wonderful man," she rubbed Don's arm, "that horrible chapter of my life is over. *Over*, thank God!"

Less than an hour later, Don and Mary pulled through the Jungle Cargo archway in the old blue truck, bound for Trujillo, waving at everyone as they drove away, honking the horn.

Brandon chuckled as he sipped another cup of coffee. "You pulled off another miracle," he said to Andrea. "Never in a million years would I have believed there was a decent woman buried beneath the façade that was Sad Mary. And the most shocking part is that she ain't that bad looking. It's like some kind of a miraculous transformation. From old hag, to a lady, in one fell swoop! Wow!"

"Remember what I told you a long time ago?"

"You told me a lot of things. What thing are you referring to?"

"Love, that single, almost indescribable thing, is the most powerful force on earth. Bar none. The transformation of Mary Thompson is just one example.

Brandon stared at Andrea, but said nothing. He just let a slow smile spread across his face.

"It feels good to help people," Andrea said. "So, speaking of that, what are we going to do about this situation with Lorenzo?"

Brandon shook his head. "You're asking me? You're asking the wrong person. I don't have a clue. What we need is another one of your miracles."

"Miracle. Yes. A miracle. I think it might solve the problem if you were to fly down here about once every couple of months or so."

"What for? Just to hold his hand and tell him I care? Come on, Andrea."

"No, there has to be a valid reason for it, or it wouldn't work. Lorenzo doesn't want to be babied. On the other hand, he is a very devoted person."

Just then, Naja came up the steps to the deck, followed closely by Cisco. Both cats came over to Brandon and plopped down on the deck.

"Well where have you two been?" Brandon asked, as he looked at the two magnificent animals.

Just then, someone came running from the compound, climbing the stairs, yelling frantically, "Lorenzo, a yellow beard bit him!"

"What?" Brandon said in alarm, rising from his chair and scrambling down the stairs. He ran toward the compound as fast as he could, yelling for Andrea to get the antivenin kit from the refrigerator.

He found Lorenzo sitting up, on the ground, holding his left wrist.

"Where'd he get you? Brandon asked, as he used his belt to make a tourniquet around Lorenzo's arm.

"Below my left thumb" Lorenzo said, obviously frightened. No doubt, the image of the Indian boy in the Mosquitia was still vivid in his mind.

"I didn't know there was a pinche' snake in the bag. I thought it was a parrot. Fucking Indian just stood there, never warned me or anything."

"Yeah, well, I'll take care of that sonofabitch, but later. Right now, I need for you to stay as calm as possible."

Andrea arrived with the antivenin kit. Brandon began

mixing the antivenin powder in the syringe as quickly as he could.

"Take my knife and cut across both fang marks," Brandon said to Andrea. There's a suction cup in this kit somewhere. Suck as much of that poison out of there as you can."

By now, the girls had arrived. Brandon looked around and saw them. "Anna Maria, call the hospital. Get a Medi-vac helicopter out here. I don't care who you have to threaten, just get it here, pronto. Suyapa, go get me a bucket filled with ice and water, half and half. Do it *now*!"

"Am I going to die, Jefe? Lorenzo asked.

"Not if I have anything to say about it," Brandon said. "You try to do something dumb like that and I'll kick your Honduran ass." Then, the injection was ready. "Mira," Brandon said, "this is going to hurt a bit, but it's the thing that will save your life, so just hang in there, okay?"

Lorenzo nodded. Brandon inserted the needle just under the skin, all the way, slowly injecting the antivenin, then repeated, making a 'belt' of the lifesaving antidote around Lorenzo's arm. After that was done, he mixed a second vial and injected it into the muscle of the upper arm.

Lorenzo tried to lie down. "No," Brandon said. "You can't do that. We need to keep your hand below the level of your heart.

Several Indians were standing around watching but doing nothing to help. Brandon looked up at them and barked, "Get out of here. Go home. Wait! I want to know who brought the snake.

Of all the Indians present, only one of them pointed at the man who had brought the cardboard box containing the snake in the bag. Brandon stood up and hit the man with all his fury, sending the Indian flying backwards where he hit the side of the store-room, then crumpled to the ground, unconscious.

"Now," Brandon said, furious, "The rest of you piss ants get out of here, before I do the same to you."

With that, the gathering of campocinos scattered as fast as they could move.

"Idiots!" Brandon said, then squatted back down to tend to Lorenzo. Suyapa had returned with the ice slush, but Andrea was still suctioning blood out of the wound.

Anna Maria came scrambling down the back steps, yelling. "The helicopter is on the way! The helicopter is on the way!"

"Good," Brandon said. "Thank you, Anna Maria. You did a fine job" By now, both girls were sobbing in fear. They loved Lorenzo like a brother. They had known him their entire lives. To see him with his life threatened was almost more than they could bear.

By now, despite the antivenin, Lorenzo's left arm was beginning to swell up as if an air hose had been pumping air into him.

"Chingow! It hurts, Jefe." Lorenzo said, his eyes wide with fear.

"I know, mi hijo. The Medi-vac chopper is on the way. It'll be here in just a minute. We'll get your skinny ass to the hospital. Looking at all those nurses will take your mind off the pain."

In less than three minutes, the sound of a helicopter approaching could be heard above the palm trees. A moment later it was in sight, looking for a place to land. When it was on the ground the bay door slid open and two white uniformed men jumped out, grabbed a stretcher and ran toward Lorenzo.

Moments later, he was loaded onto the stretcher and being wheeled toward the chopper. Brandon and Andrea followed along. Brandon shouted instructions to the girls and also told them to stay close by the phone for updates.

Brandon didn't ask, he simply jumped into the chopper and

pulled Andrea in behind him. He was not going to leave Lorenzo's side for a moment.

———

A couple of hours later, in the waiting room of the hospital, Brandon and Andrea sat nervously waiting for some news. A doctor finally emerged from the operating room to speak with them. His name was Dr. Emilio Contreras. He approached Brandon and Andrea, who stood up when they saw him coming.

"Lorenzo is alive, for now." He looked at both Brandon, and then Andrea. "You saved his life. Both of you. If you hadn't gotten some of that venom out of him, we wouldn't be having this conversation. And of course, knowing how to inject that anti-venin made all the difference in the world."

"So, what are his chances?" Andrea asked.

"I'd say they're pretty good, as long as gangrene doesn't set in. But that isn't really a problem with fer-de-lance bites. All depends on keeping the circulation going."

Then Dr. Contreras looked at Brandon. "You were a friend of Dr. Dominguez, right?"

"What do you mean, 'were'?" Brandon countered.

"Well, everyone I know assumes he is dead. I mean, the man disappeared in the middle of the night from that cantina. He hasn't been seen or heard from since. What do you think happened to him?"

Brandon looked at Andrea, then at the doctor. "Well, yes, Doc is a friend, so obviously I have to hope for a positive outcome."

"Yes, yes. I understand. I guess being a doctor, maybe I need to get away from this hospital a little more."

"Can we go in and see Lorenzo?" Andrea asked.

"Just as soon as they move him to a room. He'll be in ICU for several days."

"Of course," Andrea said.

The doctor then shook hands and excused himself.

As Brandon and Andrea regained their seats, Andrea whispered, "I knew that was going to happen, sooner or later."

"What?"

"Somebody bringing up Doc."

Brandon smiled slightly. "'Bringing up' might not be the best choice of words."

Andrea gave him a look but said nothing.

An hour later, Lorenzo was wheeled out of the ER to ICU. He had a ventilator tube down his throat and an IV in both arms. He was asleep, Brandon assumed from a sedative administered for the pain.

He was placed in a dormitory style room. Brandon immediately raised hell. "Are you telling me there are no private rooms for ICU?

"Yes, Mister Shaw. But they are more expensive. We thought,"

"You thought? No, you didn't. You didn't think at all or you would have come to me and asked. Now, get his ass out of here and into a private room, and I am assuming you have around the clock nurses to watch over him?"

"If you wish."

"Wish? I demand it. Get him moved right this minute or let me see the administrator of this dog pound."

"We will move him to our very best room immediately."

"You'd better!" Brandon was yelling. Andrea was trying to calm him down. But he was too concerned about Lorenzo to be calm. Brandon started yelling again, loud enough to be heard in half the hospital.

"This man will receive the very best care this hospital has to offer, or somebody is gonna get fired. You hear me?"

"Yes, Mr. Shaw," the ER nurse said, obviously somewhat intimidated. "We only want what's best for him too."

Brandon calmed down a little. "All right. That's more like it. We're also going to need roll-away beds in there because we are *not* leaving his side."

"Yes, of course."

Lorenzo didn't look good. His left arm was swollen so badly that it didn't look like an arm, and he was pale. He was also asleep, which was too bad, because he missed all the fuss Brandon had put up. He would think, 'Don Brandon is in fine tune! He really loves me!'

Brandon stood on one side of Lorenzo's bed, Andrea on the other.

"You got your cell phone?" he asked Andrea. She nodded yes.

"I didn't think to grab mine in all the rush. You want to call the girls and give them an update? I know they're worried sick."

Andrea reached for her phone and called the compound. A very worried Anna Maria answered. Andrea, speaking in a soft voice, filled her in on the latest status. Anna Maria thanked her, then added, "Naja and Cisco know something is wrong. They keep roaring. It is very loud, and they won't stop."

Andrea relayed this information to Brandon. He said, "Tell Anna Maria to go talk to Naja. She has known Naja since she was a tiny cub. Naja will understand and calm down."

———

A couple of hours after dark, Don and Mary showed up. Brandon and Andrea were sitting in chairs close to either side of Lorenzo's bed. There was an ER nurse standing adjacent to the head of the bed, keeping a close eye on the read-out of electronic instruments now hooked up to Lorenzo.

"What's the prognosis?" Mary asked.

Andrea proceeded to give Mary and Don a run-down of everything they knew up to the moment. Mary then moved to the foot of the bed and gently touched Lorenzo's feet. Her gentle touch made Lorenzo stir. He managed to open his eyes. Brandon spotted it immediately.

"You're in the hospital," he said softly to Lorenzo. "Don't try to talk. You've got a ventilator tube down your throat. This is for extra safety in case your lungs collapse from the venom. But that hasn't happened, so we're very hopeful. It was a nasty bite, but I believe you're going to survive. You'd better, because I don't want to have to train another compound manager, and there's a lot of shit to do out there."

"We are all here for you, Lorenzo," Andrea said. "Me, Brandon, Mary and Don. Brandon and I will not leave your side until this is over. We promise. Oh! And the girls send their love. They are praying for you."

"That's right," Brandon added. "You don't have to worry about a thing in the world except getting well."

"Hi, Lorenzo," Mary said from the foot of the bed. Don and I will be here to watch over you also. Oh! You need to know that Naja and Cisco are very upset that you aren't at Jungle Cargo. You need to get well so you can go see them. We'd like to bring them here, but that may not go over too well."

It was about midnight when buzzers and other alarms started sounding. Brandon had started to doze in his chair, Don was awake, listening to the conversation going on between Andrea and Mary.

The nurse on duty read the instruments and then pressed the call button. "Room three, code blue. Room three, code blue."

Moments later, a loud buzzer started sounding. Lorenzo's heart had stopped. Within moments, a medical team entered the room led by a rather large man that was in the mood for no bullshit.

"Everybody, get out of this room, now!" he said, as they ripped the sheets off of Lorenzo's chest area. A defibrillator was wheeled in, gel placed on the paddles and then the signal "*Clear!*" given by the large man. He held the paddles against Lorenzo's chest and hit the button. A loud 'thump' was heard. A nurse held a stethoscope to Lorenzo's chest and listened. After a few moments, she shook her head, no, and backed off. The defib machine was recharged and the paddles reapplied to Lorenzo's chest.

"*Clear*! - Thump!" Again, the nurse listened, and the large medical tech watched the read-out on the screen. After several moments, she nodded yes. Most of the medical techs started to leave the room.

The big tech stopped in front of Brandon as he made his exit. "There are too many people in this room. Some of you need to go home. No more than two visitors in here."

Brandon got nose to nose with the tech. "You did a fine job in there. Don't fuck it up by trying to push us around, or I'll put you in a bed next to Lorenzo. You understand? I'm not in the mood to be trifled with. We are all people who love Lorenzo, and we aren't going anywhere."

"I'm going to call the hospital administrator," the large tech said as he stared at Brandon, only inches away from him.

"Good," Brandon said. "You do that. And if that fudge packer comes in here trying to throw his weight around, I'll whip his ass and put him in a bed right next to you. Are we clear yet?"

The med tech caved in. There was suddenly fear in his eyes. "I believe so," he muttered.

"Fantastic," Brandon said. "Have a nice day."

With that, Brandon dismissed the med tech and walked back into Lorenzo's room. He was slowly followed by Andrea,

Mary and Don. Don was keeping one eye on the retreating med tech to see what he was going to do. But apparently, Brandon's keel hauling had been effective. The only thing the med tech did was to retreat behind the desk at the nurse's station and whisper to a female co-hort.

"Pussy!" Don thought.

CHAPTER TEN

The Power Of Love

In three days' time, the ventilator was removed from Lorenzo's throat. Even so, Lorenzo could not talk. Not at first, anyway. But he wanted to very badly. What he did do was manage to raise the head of the bed up high, then reach out to hug everyone. Tears flowed down his cheeks, bespeaking what he wanted to say. His arm was still swollen but receding.

The hospital had been feeding him intravenously, but now he was making hand signs that he wanted something to eat. This was very good news.

The smiling nurse said, "I can get you some warm broth. That's all you can have right now because your throat is going to be very sore."

When she left the room, Lorenzo looked around at all four of his visitors. His expression said it all. He extended his right arm toward each one of them and although silent, his lips said, "Thank you. I love you."

"We love you too, Lorenzo," Andrea said, taking Lorenzo's outstretched hand and squeezing it.

Brandon smiled down at him. "It looks like you're out of the woods, big guy. Now it's just going to be a matter of a slow train back. They tell us you're going to have to 'convalesce' for at least three months. You know, I think I have seen just how far you're willing to go to sit around on your ass and let people wait on you!"

Lorenzo attempted a smile.

"Yeah," Don added. "We're interviewing nurses now to come take care of you at Jungle Cargo. But there are special requirements. Right, Brandon?"

"That's right. Let's see, first, she has to weigh at least three hundred pounds."

"Secondly, she has to have a face like a howler monkey," Don added.

"Right again," Brandon said. "We've discussed this. Put a lot of thought into it. What else was it, Don? She has to smell like a rotten watermelon."

"Yep. And scratch herself a lot."

"Hair that looks like she raises pigeons in it. Oh! And no shaved legs or armpits."

"Underwear that would stick to the ceiling if she threw them up there."

"To draw the flies away from herself," Brandon said. "Anything else, Don?"

"Oh yeah, she has to have a voice like a wrestler."

"Right! I almost forgot that part. And then we're going to set you up out on the deck in your favorite chair, feed you warm beer, no limes of course. And for every meal, chilaquiles. The kind they make in Oaxaca that will burn a hole through a lava rock mocajete."

"See, we figure that way, you will probably 'rehabilitate' faster and get back on the job. Of course, you could always hire your special nurse to follow you around, farting, to help keep you moving a little faster."

Lorenzo looked at Andrea imploringly and did a hand motion indicating he wanted something to write with. Andrea pulled a small pad and pen from the drawer in the bedside table. She handed it to Lorenzo, who jotted a quick note which read,

"Please, don't take me out of this hospital!"

Everyone laughed. Mary made her way to the head of the bed and gave Lorenzo a long, warm hug.

CHAPTER ELEVEN

Return to Jungle Cargo

ALMOST THREE MONTHS PASSED BEFORE LORENZO LEFT THE hospital. There had been numerous complications, most of which were not life threatening, but at one point the amputation of his left arm was considered. Brandon Shaw, feeling almost helpless, called in a specialist from the United States to intercede. Because of the specialist's efforts, the arm was saved, and so was Lorenzo's life, as well as his dignity.

It was a happy moment when they pulled up in front of the house at Cuyamel. Lorenzo, still sitting in the Jeep, looked up at the house and said, "Hijo! It is so good to be home. I wondered if I would ever see this place again."

The girls came scrambling down the stairs and were all over Lorenzo, covering him with hugs and kisses, and cooing, telling him how glad they were to have him home. Lorenzo could not restrain his impish smile. It was a glorious home coming.

But Lorenzo was still weak. He had to be helped up the stairs. The first place he wanted to go was out onto the front deck. Once seated, he smiled broadly and looked around, as if this was the first time he had ever seen this place.

By now, Don Houseman had dried in the house that he was building. He and Mary were a solid, close couple. As for Mary, she was completely unrecognizable from the Sad Mary of Trujillo. The couple were living in Don's modern, and fairly spacious RV, while they worked on the house.

Don had managed to meet and pay off Mr. Serna, and therefore got a power line run from the transformer at Jungle Cargo, through the trees to his property.

Brandon and Andrea filled Lorenzo in on all this and any other news. The girls let him know everything that had transpired in Sambala. Before long, Lorenzo had been briefed and felt like he was up to speed.

"When you get your strength back," Brandon was saying, "You'll need to rebuild a relationship with these Indians around here. We thought I was going to be something of a pariah after clobbering the asshole that brought the snake. But it didn't turn out that way after all. He became the pariah among his own people. From what I heard the other hunters got really pissed at the guy for fucking up a good deal for them. Nobody will have anything to do with him anymore."

"Meanwhile," Andrea added, "we're going to have some changes when it comes to intake policy. You do not reach in and grab anything anymore, ever. The hunter who brings it here must extract it from whatever they bring it in and present it to you so you can examine it clearly before ever touching it. And when possible, you don't ever touch it at all. For instance, if it's a parrot, the hunter will place it in a little sali-port that we built on the side of the intake cage, and the parrot will be moved into the cage, proper."

"No more chances of being bitten by anything," Brandon said.

"Not even parrots," Andrea added.

Anna Maria came to the table with tall glasses of iced tea for everyone. Lorenzo looked at the tea a little suspiciously.

"No beer," Andrea explained. Not until you get a little stronger.

"There's another little matter," Brandon said. "There are two jaguars downstairs in their run that want to see you very badly. Do you think you can handle it?"

"Of course, I can," Lorenzo said enthusiastically. "I have missed them so much."

"Alright. I'm going to go let them out of their run, but brace yourself!"

Lorenzo laughed, but then said, "Before you go, Jefe, I want to tell you about a dream I had."

"A dream?"

"Yeah. It was right after we made it to the hospital. I was passed out, probably close to buying my ticket. In my dream, I woke up in The Lost City of The Monkey God. I was on top of a pyramid. You were there. Only, you looked different, and Jefe, you had claws for hands. Big, hairy, mother fucking paws with razor sharp claws. La verdad! Anyway, you looked at me and you said, 'Lorenzo, you cannot stay. You have to go back to your world. Go now!' That's what you said, Jefe. Plain as I am sitting here, I saw you. That dream was very real. It was like, more than a dream. It was a pinche' view into the beyond. I don't know how to explain it. But I think it's the reason I lived. Because you told me I couldn't stay in that world where you were. I just thought you'd like to know."

Brandon looked over at Andrea, then back at Lorenzo. "Thank you, Lorenzo. Yes. I'm very glad you told me." Then Brandon turned and walked down the steps to go get Naja and Cisco.

Andrea sat in her chair, silent and somewhat stunned by Lorenzo's revelation about his dream. She wondered briefly just how close they might be living to an alter world where time is over a thousand years in the past.

A couple of minutes later and there was noise on the steps

beside the deck. How ironic, Andrea mused. Another place, somebody else would probably have a heart attack if they saw two jaguars coming at them. Here, in the world of Brandon Shaw, it was nothing unusual, and was a thing of love. How could anybody help but to love this man?

First Naja, then Cisco, arrived on the landing and rushed over to Lorenzo who by now was in tears when he saw these magnificent animals. They rubbed on his legs and made purring noises. Lorenzo rubbed them back and hugged them as best he could, with his right arm. They had obviously been instructed to not overwhelm the man. But once the animal greeting settled down, both big cats took up places on either side of Lorenzo and laid down on the deck. Lorenzo was protected against any danger that might approach.

Don and Mary also showed up. They had been notified that Lorenzo was coming home and had been invited to a celebratory lunch on the deck. It was a surprise for Lorenzo's homecoming. Minimal cooking was involved because Brandon had arranged everything in town. Food was brought in, and caterers to serve it. Then, a trio of musicians came up the stairs and began playing. More guests arrived including Don Julio from next door who rented horses.

The biggest surprise was when personnel from the hospital began to arrive. This included the big med tech that Brandon had keel hauled the first night Lorenzo was in the hospital. There was eating, dancing, talking, relaxing. Lorenzo couldn't believe his eyes.

"All this is for me?"

"Yep," Brandon said. "We're glad to have you home, you little snot. I hate to admit it, but I don't know what any of us would do without you around here," Brandon said. Everyone who was gathered around Lorenzo agreed in unison. And then, the three cantadores sang a song which they called, "The Ballad of Lorenzo Ponce."

It had a somewhat 'heroic' feel to it and the words declared that Lorenzo was a man who walked with jaguars and not even the deadly, feared 'quatro narises' (four noses: fer-de-lance) could kill him. The guitar strummed, the bugle blasted, and the string base added bottom. It was a beautiful song, sung with heart. Lorenzo, sitting in his chair, was clearly moved.

Then, a birthday cake was presented to him. "But, it's not my birthday," Lorenzo protested.

"Yes, it is," Andrea explained. "After what you've been through, are you going to deny that this is a new life you're beginning?"

"Either that, or I must be dreaming," Lorenzo said with a huge grin.

And then it happened! At that very moment, a beautiful young woman with black hair that hung to the middle of her back appeared in front of Lorenzo. She was wearing a light blue colored sun dress. But Lorenzo never saw that. As Lorenzo looked up at her, his mouth fell open. Her beauty was stunning.

"Hello, Lorenzo," she said, "my name is Leticia. I work in the lab at the hospital. I may not know you. But I certainly know your blood!" She laughed a melodic laugh and smiled sweetly. "Thanks for inviting me."

"Oh, you are most welcome," Lorenzo said, trying to stand to shake hands with the beautiful vision before him.

"Won't you please join me? Just nudge a jaguar over!" he said, an attempt at humor. Leticia did respond to Lorenzo's jest and sat in a chair next to him.

She looked at Naja and Cisco. "They are very beautiful. May I pet them?"

"I'm sure they would love that," Lorenzo answered. He sneaked a look at Andrea, standing on the other side of the deck, next to Brandon, then raised his eyebrows a couple of times.

Watching from across the deck, Brandon turned to Andrea and asked, "Andrea?"

"What? Well, don't you think it's about time that Lorenzo settled down and, well, you know."

"So, you did do this?"

"Maybe I had 'a little' to do with it. Just a little. All I did was invite the lady to our party. Can I help it if she thinks Lorenzo is a hero?" she said coyly, as only a woman can do.

Brandon shook his head and smiled. "You are truly amazing. I wonder how I ever got along without you?"

"Not too well, from what I saw."

"No, not too well at all. And I damn sure don't know what I would do without you now."

"So, I take that to mean, you don't want to find out?"

"No. I absolutely do not want to find out."

———

It was late afternoon when the party started to break-up. People said their goodbyes until the only ones left were Don and Mary, and Leticia who was so locked in conversation with Lorenzo that she seemed oblivious to anything else that was going on around her.

That is, until Naja struggled to her feet and wobbled over to the patio doors. She didn't try to go into the house, but rather plopped down near the wall of the house and laid on her side.

"Something is wrong with Naja!" Andrea said, alarmed.

Brandon rushed to Naja's side, got down on his knees and placed her head in his lap. She was panting hard.

"What's the matter girl?" Brandon beseeched. "Where does it hurt?"

Naja looked into Brandon's eyes, but there was no sound. The girls started crying. Lorenzo struggled to get down beside her. Cisco seemed unworried, and this was suddenly a clue for Brandon.

"Wait a minute!" he said. "Naja isn't sick." He told the girls to go quickly and get some old blankets. They rushed inside, returning with the blankets moments later.

Andrea's mouth opened wide once the truth hit her. "Is what I think is going to happen, about to happen?"

Brandon looked up at her. "It all depends. What do you think is about to happen?"

"You're not having a conniption. And if Naja was in pain or danger you would be. So, my guess is, a little miracle is about the happen. Right?"

"I believe that to be the case, yes. Looks like Cisco is more than a friend, I think he is Naja's husband."

Sure enough, within the next hour, Naja gave birth to not one, but two tiny jaguar cubs. Their eyes were shut, and they mewed for their mommy. One was as black as night, just like Naja. And it was a female. The other was a little rosetted male that was the spitting image of his father.

Brandon Shaw smiled a very gentle, fatherly smile. But there were tears of joy that managed to find their way down his cheeks. Tears which he quickly wiped away. When he regained his composure, he stood and said, "Anybody here who tells someone they saw me 'almost' crying and I'll break their neck, I don't care who it is."

"Your secret is safe with us," Don said.

Brandon bent over and asked Naja if he could hold her cubs for a minute. He picked up the male and handed it to Andrea, then picked up the female and cradled it against his body, next to his heart.

"Gather around, everybody. Lorenzo, keep your seat. You, Leticia, stay right where you are. Everybody, gather around them."

When everyone had moved to form a tight group in front

of Brandon and Andrea, Brandon got a very strange, yet proud look on his face.

Smiling a smile of peace and pride, he said to the group, very proudly, "Ladies and gentlemen; Behold! These two jaguar cubs are not just jaguar cubs. In this most special moment, they are a symbol, and more special than words can convey. They represent love. They represent hope. They represent, renewal. And, they represent the perpetuation and the continuation of Jungle Cargo. Om mani padme hum! So be it, and let it be known to all present."

Brandon held the tiny jaguar cub close to his chest, ever so tenderly, and looked at Andrea in a way she had never seen before.

"You're right," he said to Andrea. "Love is the most powerful force on earth. You've taught me sooo much, sweet woman."

"Yeah," she said approvingly. "Like what?"

"Because of you," he said with love in his eyes, "I can see tomorrow."

THE END

———

Don't miss out on your next favorite book!
Join the Melange Books mailing list at
www.melange-books.com/mail.html

THANK YOU FOR READING

Did you enjoy this book?

We invite you to leave a review at your favorite book site, such as Goodreads, Amazon, Barnes & Noble, etc.

DID YOU KNOW THAT LEAVING A REVIEW...

- Helps other readers find books they may enjoy.
- Gives you a chance to let your voice be heard.
- Gives authors recognition for their hard work.
- Doesn't have to be long. A sentence or two about why you liked the book will do.

ABOUT THE AUTHOR

GEORGE DISMUKES spent the first half of his life in pursuit of adventure. This ranged from bullfighting as a youth to milking poisonous snakes professionally at Ross Allen's Reptile Institute in Silver Springs, Florida. The early 60s found him pursuing wild animals across the Serengeti in the movie business and operating an animal export company in Iquitos, Peru.

He spent many years exploring archaeological sites of the ancient Maya Indians in Central America and studying their lost civilization. He also lived in Honduras, where the story, TWO FACES OF THE JAGUAR, and THE LOST CITY take place.

In 1980, he began a video production company in Houston, Texas and worked as a 'triple threat' (writer/director/producer) creating some of the Houston market's most creative television commercials. He won a CLEO award for his production of a series of television PSAs concerning prevention of child abuse, funded through a grant from the University of Houston.

Currently, he lives on the Texas Coast with his soul mate and closest friend, Nadine, where he writes and works in magazine advertising. His hobbies include growing exotic chili peppers and experimenting with salsa recipes. Above all, George is a devout animal lover and advocate, fighting against animal abuse. He has two dogs, named Pulga and Gizmo, respectively.

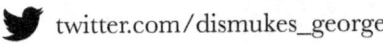 twitter.com/dismukes_george

ALSO BY GEORGE DISMUKES

Two Faces of the Jaguar